William Cornelius Reichel, John G. E. Heckewelder

Names Which the Lenni Lennape or Delaware Indians Gave

to Rivers

streams and localities, within the states of Pennsylvania, New Jersey,

Maryland, and Virginia, with their significations

William Cornelius Reichel, John G. E. Heckewelder

Names Which the Lenni Lennape or Delaware Indians Gave to Rivers
streams and localities, within the states of Pennsylvania, New Jersey, Maryland, and Virginia, with their significations

ISBN/EAN: 9783337301842

Printed in Europe, USA, Canada, Australia, Japan

Cover: Foto ©Andreas Hilbeck / pixelio.de

More available books at **www.hansebooks.com**

NAMES

WHICH THE

LENNI LENNAPE OR DELAWARE INDIANS

GAVE TO

RIVERS, STREAMS AND LOCALITIES,

WITHIN THE STATES OF

PENNSYLVANIA, NEW JERSEY, MARYLAND and VIRGINIA,

WITH THEIR SIGNIFICATIONS.

PREPARED FOR THE TRANSACTIONS OF THE
MORAVIAN HISTORICAL SOCIETY FROM
A MS. BY JOHN HECKEWELDER,

BY

WILLIAM C. REICHEL.

BETHLEHEM:
H. T. CLAUDER, PRINTER.
1872.

NAMES WHICH THE LENNI LENNAPE OR DELAWARE INDIANS GAVE TO RIVERS, STREAMS AND LOCALITIES WITHIN THE STATES OF PENNSYLVANIA, NEW JERSEY, MARYLAND AND VIRGINIA, WITH THEIR SIGNIFICATIONS, BY JOHN HECKEWELDER.

The footprints of extinct races of men always become objects of interest in proportion to the fewness of their number and the obscurity of their character. Those of the Indian tribes, who once dwelt along the rivers that drain the loveliest portions of the eastern slope of the Appalachians, are growing less and fainter with the lapse of succeeding years. With no records to perpetuate the story of their origin, the course of migratory waves, the wars of contending nations, the rise and decadence of clans and the prowess of national heroes and heroines, save an oral tradition distorted by the adornments of a rude poesy,—the archæology of this occidental people is likely to remain a sealed book. Even the tokens they have left us in enduring stone,—memorial pillars, implements of war, of the chase and of the household,—whether inscribed in hieroglyphics of hidden meaning, or cunningly wrought from material as hard as adamant in an age which was ignorant of the use of the metals,—instead of aiding in the solution of the problem, present it in a more perplexing form. Equally obscure and unintelligible, but for the interpreter through whom they now speak, would have forever remained another class of relics come down to us—we mean the straggling footprints of its language, impressed upon the beautiful objects of nature among which this mysterious people lived and passed away.

It is with such fragmentary remains of a now dead tongue that this paper is concerned; principally with words belonging to the euphonious dialect of the Unamis or Delawares of the lowlands, the first of the copper-colored aborigines, who witnessed the advent of the white man from countries beyond the "great water," and the rising of the sun.

When Mr. Heckewelder undertook to restore the mutilated forms of Indian appellations of mountains, rivers and localities current among the whites of his time, and then to point out their significance, he did a work for which he is entitled to grateful remembrance. These names are now no longer empty sounds. They have become as it were living things, endowed with the faculty of speech. Transformed by him into tutelary spirits, they cling like dryads and hamadryads to the inanimate objects to which they were long ago attached, and keep watch over the artless records inscribed upon them by another race of men. Some fix the localities of events that belong to the history of nations or of incidents that occurred in the experience of individuals,—some the favorite haunts of the animals of the chase or the habitat of those spontaneous products of nature which ministered to the Indian's daily wants; others afford us glimpses of his sylvan life when on the hunt or on the war-path, or are descriptive of peculiarities in the landscape, of its flora or of its fauna; while together they people portions of our country with historical recollections of their former occupants which would otherwise have been inevitably lost.

In preparing this paper, the editor took some liberties with Mr. Heckewelder's MS., deeming it desirable to avoid repetitions, to abbreviate modes of expression where it could be done without involving a sacrifice of the compiler's meaning, and to adapt topographical descriptions to the geography of the present day. An alphabetical arrangement of the names suggested itself at once as the most convenient for reference. The historical annotations were drawn from a variety of trustworthy sources, and whilst in their selection preference was given to such matter as belongs to Moravian history, the attempt was made in all cases to adduce the earliest use or mention on record of the names under consideration. The following maps were freely consulted in this effort: 1st. "*A Map of the Middle British Colonies in America and of Aquanishuonigy, the Country of the Confederate Indians, comprehending Aquanishuonigy proper, their place of residence,* (that part of the State of New York lying south of the Mohawk)—*Ohio* (embracing the region of country south of the Maumee as far down as the Kentucky) and *Tiuxsoxruntie* (the country north of the Maumee and west of the Huron, as high as Lake Huron) *their deer-hunting countries,*—and *Couxsaxrage* (upper New York, south of the St.

Lawrence) and *Skaniadarade* (the country lying north of Lake Erie) *their beaver-hunting country;*" "published by Act of Parliament by Lewis Evans, June 22, 1755, and sold by R. Dodsley in Pall Mall, London, and by the author in Philadelphia. Engraved by James Turner, of Philadelphia." Being dedicated to the Honble Thomas Pownall, Esq., the map is illuminated with the coat of arms of the Pownall family, blazoned as follows: *Arms.* Arg., a lion rampant, sa. charged on the breast with a cross paté of the first. *Crest.* A lion's jambe crased, erect ppr, grasping a key or, from which a chain is reflexed of the last. 2. "*A Map of the improved part of the Province of Pennsylvania, humbly dedicated to the Hon. Thomas Penn and Richard Penn, Esqrs., true and absolute Proprietaries and Governors of the Province of Pennsylvania, and Counties of New Castle, Kent and Sussex on Delaware, by Nicholas Scull,* and published according to Act of Parliament, January 1, 1759." The formula of dedication appearing on this invaluable historical chart is inscribed within elaborate scroll-work, surrounded by the arms and crest of the Penn family blazoned thus: *Arms.* Arg. on a fess sa. three plates. *Crest,* A demi-lion rampant, ppr. gorged with a collar sa. charged with three plates. *Motto.* Mercy and Justice. 3. "*A Map of the State of Pennsylvania, by Reading Howell. Respectfully inscribed to Thomas Mifflin, Governor, and to the Senate and House of Representatives of the Commonwealth of Pennsylvania by the author. Published August 1, 1792, for him, and sold by James Phillips, George's Yard, Lombard Street, London.*" This map is beautifully executed, and shows, to use the words of the draftsman, "the triangle lately purchased by Congress, and the boundary lines of the State as run by the respective Commissioners, with parts of Lake Erie and Presqu' Isle; also by actual survey the rivers Susquehanna (its north-east and west branches), Tyoga, Sinnemahoning, Juniata, Lehigh, Lexawacsein, Schuylkill, and the western rivers, Ohio, Alleghany, Conewango,—part of the Chautaughque Lake and French Creek, agreeable to the late discoveries,—the Monaungahela, Yaxhiogeni and Kiskemanetas; also the larger creeks, most of the lesser streams, mountains, the principal old roads, with the many new ones in the northern and western parts of the State, and portages and communications according to the late surveys by order of Government; furthermore the division

lines of the respective counties and townships, a delineation of the
districts of depreciation and donation lands, with all the other districts in the new purchase—besides the seats of justice in the respective counties, iron-works, mills, manufactories, locations of
minerals, bridle-roads, Indian-paths, &c., &c."

It was from a third edition of this map, that Mr. Heckewelder,
as he tells us, copied the majority of names in his catalogue;
Proud's History of Pennsylvania (Phila. 1798) furnished him
with a few, and his friend Samuel D. Franks, of Harrisburg, with
those occurring in Indian deeds preserved in the Land Office of
the Commonwealth.

David Zeisberger's "*Essay of a Delaware Indian and English
Spelling-book for the use of the Christian Indians on the Muskingum*" (Phila. 1776) supplied the vocables which are incorporated
in the notes for the purpose of confirming or illustrating Heeke-
welder's interpretation.

In conclusion, it may be stated that the Moravian missionaries
of the last century were unanimous in pronouncing the Unami
dialect of the Delaware, despite its many gutturals and aspirates,
eminently musical, and well adapted by its structure to the purposes of public harangue or oratory. A German tongue, they add,
finds no difficulty in mastering even its characteristic sounds, and
enjoys the advantage of meeting with vowels that differ as to
their power, in no respect from those with which it is already
familiar. The absence of the consonants *r*, *f*, and *v*, the accumu-
lation of the *k* sounds (all enunciated from the depths of the throat),
the paucity of monosyllabic and the abundance of compound and
polysyllabic words, are marked peculiarities of this dialect. The .
last feature renders its acquisition extremely difficult. Finally,
it should be kept in mind that in words of three syllables, the
stress of the voice *generally* falls upon the penult; in polysyllables,
however, *always;* and that a violation of rules of accent, in most
cases, involves an entire change of signification.

John G. E. Heckewelder, missionary to the Delawares, was born
March 12, 1743, in Bedford O. E. whither his father (who was a
native of Moravia), had been sent from Herrnhut, a few years previous, to labor in the service of the Brethren's Church. His child-
hood was spent at the Brethren's schools at Buttermere, in Wilts,
and at Smith-house and Fulneck in Yorkshire. In 1754 he accom-

panied his parents to Bethlehem, whence, on leaving school, he was placed at Christian's Spring, where he engaged in the labors of the farm, then worked by the young men of the settlement for the benefit of their Economy. He was next indentured to William Nixon a cedar-cooper at Bethlehem. It was while thus employed that the desire he had for some time felt of becoming an evangelist to the Indians was gratified, as in the spring of 1762 he was called to accompany Frederick Post, who had planned a mission among the tribes of the far west, to the Tuscarawas branch of the Muskingum. But the Pontiac war broke out, and the adventurous attempt was abandoned before the expiration of the year.

In the interval between 1763 and 1771, Mr. Heckewelder was occasionally dispatched from his cooper's shop in the capacity of a messenger or runner in the service of the mission, to Friedens-hütten on the Wyalusing, and to Indian towns on the Susquehanna. The most active period of his life, however, dates from 1771, and covers an interval of fifteen years, during which he participated in the various fortunes of the Moravian Indians, accompanying them on their tedious migrations westward,—from the Susquehanna to the Allegheny, thence to the Big Beaver, and thence to the Mus-kingum, sharing their joys and their sorrows, in times of peace and war, " in journeyings often, in perils of waters, in perils of robbers, in perils of his countrymen, in perils by the heathen, in perils in the wilderness, in weariness, in watchings often, in hunger and thirst, in fastings often, in cold and nakedness;" and, yet spared as to his life to a good old age, in the quiet days of which, when rest-ing from his labors, he drew up his well known "Narrative" of eventful years in his own experience and in the history of his Church.

In the autumn of 1786, on withdrawing from active service in the mission, Mr. Heckewelder settled with his wife (Sarah, m. n. Ohneberg, whom he had married in 1780) and two daughters at Bethlehem. This change, however, brought him no rest, as much of his time for the next fifteen years was devoted to the interests of the Church and her missions, in behalf of which he undertook frequent long and trying journeys. In 1792 and 1793, Govern-ment associated him with United States Commissioners to treat for peace with the Indians of the Maumee and the Wabash. This was a high testimonial of confidence in his knowledge of Indian life and Indian affairs. The remuneration he received for these services was judiciously economized for his old age, his immediate wants being supplied by his handicraft, and the income accruing from a nursery he had planted on his return from the western country. There are orchards still standing in the vicinity of Bethlehem set out by John Heckewelder and his daughters.

In 1801 he removed with his family to Gnadenhütten on the Tuscarawas, and was a resident of the State of Ohio for nine years. Mr. Heckewelder now became a man of official business, having been entrusted by the "Society of the United Brethren for Propagating the Gospel among the Heathen,"* with the care of the reservation of 12,000 acres of land on the Muskingum, held in trust by said Society for the benefit of the Moravian Indians. He was also in the civil service, being a Postmaster and a Justice of the Peace.

In 1810 he returned to Bethlehem, built a house (still standing on Cedar Alley), planted the premises with trees and shrubs from their native forest, surrounded himself with birds and wild flowers, and through these beautiful things of nature with which they were associated in their woodland homes, sought to prolong fellowship with his beloved Indians. In 1815 he was called to mourn the departure of his wife to the eternal world.

At a time when there was a growing spirit of inquiry among men of science in the department of Indian archæology, it need not surprise us, that Mr. Heckewelder was sought out in his retirement, and called on to contribute from the store of his experience. In this way originated his intimacy with Duponceau and Wistar of the American Philosophical Society, and that career of literary labor to which he dedicated the lonely and latter years of his life. In addition to occasional essays which are incorporated in the Transactions of that Society, Mr. Heckewelder in 1818 published his well known "Account of the History, Manners and Customs of the Indian nations who once inhabited Pennsylvania and the neighboring States," a work which was received with almost unqualified approbation. Fenimore Cooper, when venturing upon a new field of romance, drew much of his inspiration from the pages of

* This Association, whose Board has its seat at Bethlehem, was incorporated in 1788.

his fascinating volume. The "Narrative of the Mission of the United Brethren among the Delaware and Mohican Indians," appeared in 1820, and in 1822, Mr. Heckewelder, at the request of members of the American Philosophical Society, made the collection of Indian appellations here offered to the reader. This was one of his last efforts; another year of suffering, and on the 30th of January, 1823, the friend of the Delawares, having lived to become a hoary old man of seventy-nine winters, passed away.

He left three daughters; Johanna Maria, born April 16, 1781, at Salem, Tuscarawas County, Ohio, (she died at Bethlehem, Sept. 19, 1868); Anna Salome, born August 13, 1784, at New Gnadenhütten on the river Huron, Michigan; (she married Joseph Rice of Bethlehem, and died January 15, 1857), and Susanna, born at Bethlehem Dec. 31, 1786; (she married J. Christian Luckenbach of Bethlehem, and died Feb. 8, 1867).

Mr. Heckewelder was a fair representative of the Moravian missionary of the last century,—one of a class of men whose time was necessarily divided betwen the discharge of spiritual and secular duties; who preached the Gospel and administered the sacraments in houses built by their own hands; who wielded the axe as well as the sword of the Spirit, and who by lives of self-denial and patient endurance, sustained a mission among the aborigines of this country in the face of disappointments and obstacles, which would have discouraged any but men of their implicit faith in the Divine power of the Christian religion.

The subject of this notice was no scholar; nor did he make any literary pretensions. Despite this, however, and although his mode of giving expression to thought is German, his writings are characterized by a pleasing simplicity of diction, and an honesty of purpose, which enlist the sympathy of the reader. It would be presumptuous to claim for him infallibility, as we know that even the best of men are led astray, or err in their search after truth. It would be as presumptuous however to deny his statements all claim to respect. Hence we do not hesitate to say, that John Heckewelder's contributions to the store of knowledge we possess respecting Indian traditions, language, manners and customs, and life and character, are worthy of the degree of regard that is usually accorded to men of intelligence, and disinterestedness of purpose, whose position permitted them to ascertain or to observe what they relate.

2

10 TRANSACTIONS OF THE

For the curious reader, we append the following enumeration of his many journeys and their distances, found among Mr. Heckewelder's private papers, in possession of Mr. Henry B. Luckenbach, of Bethlehem, a grandson.

Miles.

In October, in company of Senseman, from Huron River to Detroit,
and return by water.. 80
1784. From Huron River to Detroit, and return............................... 80
1785. Do. do. do. twice.................................... 160
1786. From Huron River the last time to Detroit, and thence to *Cayahaga*
(in NorthEastern Ohio).. 160
Thence, in the autumn, with my family, to Bethlehem.................. 420
1787. In company of Michael Jung and Weygand to Pittsburg, and return.. 640
In October, with Bro. Ettwein, by way of Staten Island to New York. 100
Return to Bethlehem, by way of Hope, New Jersey........................ 130
1788. In August to New York (for warrants), and return..................... 200
In September, in company of Matt'w Blickensderfer to Pittsburg, and
thence with Capt. Hutchins, Surveyor General, by water to Marietta,
and (after nine weeks stay) return... 910
1789. Accompanied Bro. Abraham Steiner to *Petquottink*, and return.......... 980
In September with Bro. Charles Culver to Carlisle, and return........ 230
1792. At Washington's request was commissioned by Gen. Knox, Secretary
of War, to accompany Gen. Putnam to the Wabash, and aid in
opening negotiations for a peace with the Indians—traveling thus:
From Bethlehem to Pittsburg... 320
From Pittsburg, by water, to the Wabash........................1022
Up the Wabash to Post Vincennes................................. 160
From Post Vincennes by land to the Falls of Ohio.............. 150
From the Falls of Ohio to Pittsburg................................. 705
From Pittsburg, via Bethlehem, to Philadelphia.............. 370
——2727

1793. At the request of Government, accompanied Gen. Lincoln, Col. Pick-
ering and ex-Governor Beverly Randolph, (appointed Commissioners to treat with the friendly Indians on the Miami) via Philadelphia, New York, Albany, Schenectady, Fort Stanwix, Oneida
Lake, Oswego, Niagara and Lake Erie, as far as Detroit............. 800
From Detroit, alone to Fairfield, Upper Canada and return............. 140
From Detroit to Bethlehem, as follows: across Lake Erie to Niagara—across Lake Ontario to Kingston—from Kingston down
the St. Lawrence to Montreal—thence by land to St. Johns—thence
down Lake Champlain to Skenesborough or Whitehall—thence
along the Hudson to Albany—thence by sloop to New York, and
thence to Bethlehem...1310
179-. Accompanied Jacob Eyerly as far as Pittsburg—he was on his way
to survey lands on French Creek, and return............................. 620
1797. In company of Bro. William Henry and others, to the Muskingum..... 410
From Gnadenhütten through the wilderness (accompanied part of the
way by an Indian) to Marietta... 125
Return, with Gen. Putnam (engaged in a survey) to Gnadenhütten,
and thence to the Tuscarawas Fording Place............................ 200
A second time to Marietta by water, and thence to Bethlehem........... 640
1798. Accompanied Bro. Benjamin Mortimer to Fairfield, U. C., traveling
through the Genessee country to Buffalo, thence by way of Black
Rock, Niagara Falls, Queenstown, Newark (head of Lake Ontario)
Burlington Heights, Grand River (or Brandt's Town), the Pinery,
and Monsey Town... 530
From Fairfield (in company of William Edwards and two Indians)
by way of Detroit, Brownstown, River Raisin, Miami, Old Fort,
The Rapids, Upper Sandusky, Owl Creek and Walhending to Gna-
denhütten... 270
Thence to Pittsburg, in company of Bro. Mortimer (to escort El-
dridge), and return.. 200
In the autumn, in company of Bro. Mortimer (who along with Zeis-
berger had led some Indians from Fairfield to Gnadenhütten) to
Bethlehem.. 410

Miles.

1799. To Muskingum, and return... 820
1800. Accompanied Bro. Christian Fdc. Dencke to Gnadenhütten.............. 410
Thence in the autumn to Pittsburg, and from there by way of Fort
Franklin and Meadville to La Boeuf, pursuant to commission received from the Directors of the "Society for Propagating the Gospel
among the Heathen," to view its lands on French Creek; thence via
Pittsburg to Bethlehem... 660
1801. Moved with my family to Muskingum.. 410
To Marietta, and return.. 220
1802. Do   do. 220
To Bethlehem and return, at my own expense............................. 820
1803. To Marietta, and return.. 220
In the autumn with Bro. Loskiel from Gnadenhütten to Pittsburg,
and return.. 200
1804. On official business (to appraise houses, &c.) to Zanesville and other
towns, and return.. 140
1805. To Zanesville and return. 120
1806. To   do.   (to pay taxes) and return............................... 120
Thence to Bethlehem and return via Philadelphia, at my own expense. 850
1807. To Zanesville, and return... 120
1808. To   do.   (to pay taxes) and return............................... 120
1809. Appointed by the Assembly one of three commissioners to fix two new
County seats, visiting Canton, Wooster, Richland, &c, and return... 190
To Zanesville, and return.. 120
In December, via Zanesville and New Lancaster to the Assembly sit-
ting in Ohio, and in January of 1810, return............................. 245
1810. To Zanesville (to pay taxes) and return..................................... 110
In October removed with my family to Bethlehem.......................... 410
Thereupon to Lancaster to present William Henry Killbuck's petition
to the Assemby, and return to Philadelphia............................... 190
1813. For the last time in the Western country, traveling to Gnadenhütten
by way of Pittsburg, Harmony, Beaver Town, Tuscarawas and New
Philadelphia. From Gnadenhütten to Zanesville, and return to
Bethlehem.. 955

26,257

1. DELAWARE NAMES OF RIVERS, STREAMS AND LOCALITIES IN PENNSYLVANIA.

ALLEGHENY, corrupted from *Alligéwi*—the name of a race of Indians* said to have dwelt along the river of that name,† and in

---

* Of the wars of the Lenape and Mengwe with the Alligewi, and of the discomfiture and expulsion of the latter from Alligewinink, Heckewelder records the following tradition in his History of Indian Nations. The Lenape (the Delawares), resided many hundred years ago in a far distant country in the western part of the American Continent. For some reason they determined to migrate eastward, and accordingly set out in a body. After a very long journey and many nights' encampments by the way, they at length arrived at the *Namaesi Sipu* (i. e. the *River of Fish*, the Mississippi) where they fell in with the Mengwe (the Iroquois), who were likewise emigrating from a distant country in search of new homes, and who had struck that river somewhat higher up. Spies sent out in advance by the Lenape to reconnoitre had ascertained, before the arrival of the main body of their people on the Mississippi, that the country east of it was inhabited by a very powerful nation, who had numerous large towns built on the rivers flowing through it. This was the nation of the *Alligewi*. Many wonderful things are told of them. They are said to have been remarkably tall and stout, and even of gigantic stature, far exceeding in size the tallest of the Lenape. They were likewise skilled in the arts of defensive warfare, of throwing up entrenchments and of erecting fortifications, remains of some of which are to be seen at the present day in the western country.

The Lenape, on arriving at the Mississippi, thought it prudent, before crossing the stream, to send a messenger to the Alligewi to request permission of them to settle in their neighborhood. This was refused. Instead, however, the Alligewi expressed a willingness to allow them a passage *through* their country. The Lenape accordingly began to cross the river. It was now that the Alligewi, on seeing that the strangers were a numerous people, (not to be counted by thousands), moved by fear, fell treacherously upon those who had already crossed, slew many of them, and threatened the others with annihilation' should they persist in the passage. On recovering from the surprise, the Lenape held a council, in which they considered what was best to be done, whether to retreat, or whether to measure their strength with those who had cruelly betrayed their confidence. They felt disposed to do the latter, for they were a brave people, and incensed at the loss of their kinsmen. But prudence forbade them engaging in an unequal contest, and they were about setting their faces westward, when the Mengwe, who from their encampment had been spectators of the unprovoked attack, proposed to render them assistance, to join them in a war of conquest and extermination with the Alligewi, and after its successful close, to share with them the conquered territory. "Thus," they said, "their wanderings would end, and there they would find the homes in search of which they had left the setting sun."

Having thus united their forces, the Lenape and Mengwe declared war against

Alligewinink, i. e., all the country west of the Alleghenies, drained by the tributaries of the Ohio and their numerous sources. The Shawanose called this river *Palawu-thepiki*.

APPOLACON, (emptying into the Susquehanna from the South, in Susquehanna County), corrupted from *Apelogácan*, (in Minsi Delaware *Apellochgawan*), signifying, *whence the messenger returned*.‡

AQUANSHICOLA, (emptying into the Lehigh from the north-east in Carbon County), corrupted from *Achquoanschicola*, signifying, *where we fish with the bush-net*.§

---

the Alligewi, and great battles were fought, in which many warriors fell on both sides. It was a long and bloody contest, in which quarter was neither asked nor given. The enemy stockaded their large towns and erected fortifications, which the allies besieged, and sometimes took by storm. In a certain engagement the slain were thrown together in large heaps and covered with earth,—their places of sepulture forming tumuli or mounds, that for many generations marked the site of the great battle-field. Thus hard pressed the Alligewi, seeing their destruction inevitable, withdrew from the contest, abandoned their country to the invaders, and fled down the Mississippi, never to return. Hereupon the conquerors made a division of the country, whereby the Mengwe came into possession of the lands about the great lakes and their tributary streams, the Lenape of those situate to the south, whence these gradually moved eastward, even to the Atlantic coast, until when the white man came, the Delaware or *Lenapewihittuck* (i. e., the river of the Lenape) was in the very heart of their settlements.

† The Allegheny was called by the French, on their first hostile occupation o Pennsylvania territory in 1753, "*La Belle Riviere*," a name subsequently applied to the Ohio, the former being regarded not as a tributary, but as the *main stream* of the great river of *Alligewinink*. Hence, too, Indian traders also called the river *below the Forks* the Allegheny, or else used this name and Ohio without discrimination when speaking of the great river of Western Pennsylvania. The Delawares called the Allegheny or Ohio, *Kit-hanne*, i. e., the *main stream* in its region of country, it being the same descriptive appellation by which they designated their great river of the East, i. e., the Delaware. Jonah Davenport and James Le Tort, Indian traders, in Oct., 1731, reported that on *Kittanning River* there dwelt mostly Delawares, 50 families, 100 men, with *Kykenhammo*, their chief. (See *Delaware*, *Kittanning* and *Ohio*, in this register.)

‡ *Al-lo-ga-can*, a servant, a messenger. *Zr.*

§ *Ach-quoa-ni-can* a bush-net; *ach-quo-ne-man*, to fish with a bush-net; *ach-quoa-na-u*, caught with the bush-net.—*Zr.* "As soon as the shad (*scha-wa-nam-meek*, the *south-fish*, compounded of *scha-wa-ne-u* south, and *na-mees* fish) come from the south to deposit their spawn, running up the rivers from the sea, the Indians assemble for the annual fishery. And first they build a stone dam across the stream, the two wings or walls of which converge into a pound or wooden box, perforated with holes. This is the trap. A wild grape-vine of sufficient length to reach from shore to shore is then cut, and loaded down with brush, secured at intervals of from ten to fifteen feet. This barrier is stretched across the river, perhaps a

AUGHWICK, (a tributary of the Juniata in Huntingdon County), corrupted from *Achweck*, signifying *brushy*, i. e., *overgrown with brush.**

BALD EAGLE, (emptying into the Susquehanna from the south-

---

mile above the pound, and being held in position by Indians in canoes, is slowly towed down stream. The frightened fish are driven before it back into the dam, and thence by the Indians, posted on its walls, into the pound, where they are caught by hand. As many as a thousand are known to have been taken in this way in a morning. The Delawares called March *the shad-mouth.*"—*Loskiel's History of the Moravian Mission among the North American Indians.*

The narrow valley or gorge of the Aquanshicola (written sometimes *Aquanshahales* in old deeds), was visited by Zinzendorf in July of 1742, and by missionaries from Bethlehem, until the commencement of Indian hostilities in the fall of 1755. It most have been a favorite planting-spot of the Delawares. It may have been inhabited by even an earlier race, by a race of strong men that wrought in stone as we do in wood, handling and fashioning huge blocks taken out of the mountain side, with the same ease and accuracy of design as with which are fashioned the lesser implements of war and the chase, found so plentifully along the Aquanshicola. If ever there was a relic of a "stone-age," it is the so-called "Indian mill (*tach-quoa-hoa-can*) of the Aquanschicola," now in the museum of Mr. Richard Crist of Nazareth, Pa. Of its history we know only the following: Mr. Chas. E. Buskirk of Chestnut Hill Township, now sixty-five years of age, states that in his grandfather's time the mill was discovered, partially embedded in the ground, near the foot of the mountain on the left bank of the creek, not far from the Ross Common Tavern, and at once became an object of curiosity to the neighborhood, as well as to passing travelers. In 1860, Mr. Reuben Hartzell, on whose land it lay, had it disinterred, removed and set up in front of the Tavern. Mr. Crist purchased and had it conveyed to Nazareth in Sept. of 1869. This unique piece of antiquity is wrought from a solid block of gray sandstone, and in form is a perfect frustum of a cone, with an altitude of three feet, the diameter of the lower base being the same, and that of the upper base being one foot six inches. A funnel-shaped cavity tapering down from a ten-inch to a five-inch diameter, is chiseled into the block to the depth of two feet, at which point the polished circumference shows where the stone that *ground* or *cut* the corn, revolved in its socket. From here the grist fell through a hole, nine inches square, morticed into the lower base. The weight of the block is 2185 pounds. It would almost appear as if the mill were worked by an application of the power at the extremities of levers, fitted into the upright that carried the *cutter* or *crusher* at its base, after the fashion of a capstan—that the mill was placed over a pit, and that the grist was caught in bags or other receptacles placed in the latter. The *crushing* or *cutting* stone, although lost, is well remembered by inhabitants of Ross Common.

* *A-che-we-n* bushy.—*Zr.* An Indian village of this name, mentioned in Provincial records prior to 1750, stood on *Aughwick Creek* (it is said on the site of Shirleysburg) where Fort Shirley (so named in honor of Gen. Wm. Shirley of Massachusetts) was built in 1756. George Croghan, a trader of note, and subsequently Sir Wm. Johnson's deputy in Indian affairs, resided previous to the

west in Clinton County), called by the Delawares *Wapalanewach-schiec-hánne*, i. e., *the stream of the Bald Eagle's nest.*[*]

BALD EAGLE'S NEST,[†] in Delaware, *Wapalanewachschiéchey.*

BEAVER DAM, (a branch of the Kiskiminetas in Westmoreland County), called by the Delawares *Amochkpahásink*[‡] signifying *where the beaver has shut up the stream.*

BEAVER RIVER, (a branch of the Ohio in Beaver County), in Delaware, *Amochkwri-sipu,*[§] i. e., *beaver-river,* or *Amochk-hánne,* i. e.,

---

Indian war at *Aughwick* Old Town. In Sept. of 1754, Conrad Weisser treated with the Delawares and Shawanese of the West, in behalf of the Province, at Augh-wick.

[*] *Woap-su* and *Woa-peek,* white. *Woap-a-lanne,* the bald eagle. *Wach-schie-chey,* a nest. *Han-ne,* a stream.—*Zr.*

[†] The name of an Indian village, situated above the confluence of Buffalo Run and Bald Eagle Creek (now in Centre County), and the residence of "Bald Eagle," a noted chief. Scull's map calls it simply *"The Nest."* It stood on the flats near Milesburg, on the "Indian Path from the Great Island to Ohio."

[‡] *A-mochk,* a beaver.—*Zr.*

[§] *Sipo* and *sipu,* a river. *Si-po-til* (diminutive), a creek. *Si-punk* and *Si pu-sing,* at, or, in the river.—*Zr.* The Moravian missionary, C. Frederic Post, in the summer of 1758 undertook a perilous mission in behalf of the Proprietary Govern-ment to the Delawares of Ohio,—in the course of which he penetrated the wilds of Pennsylvania to their extreme western limits. His journal appears in full in the third volume of the Archives of Pennsylvania. Accompanied by several friendly Indians, he set out from Bethlehem on the 19th of July for Fort Augusta, (Sunbury). There he took the path along the right bank of the West Branch, leading over the *Chillisquaque,* over *Muncy, Loyalsock* and *Pine Creeks,*—crossed the *Susquehanna* at the *Great Island,* and then struck one of the main Indian thor-oughfares to the West. On the 3d of July he forded *Beech Creek,* on whose left bank he came to the forks of the road. One branch led south-west along the *Bald Eagle,* past the *Nest* to *Frankstown,* and thence to the Ohio country;—the other due West to *Chinklacamoose.* Post took the latter. It led over the *Mosh-annon,* which he crossed on the 1st of August. Next day he arrived at the village of *Chinklacamoose* in the *"Clear Fields."* Hence the travelers struck a trail to the north-west, crossed *Toby's Creek* (Clarion River), and on the 7th of August reached *Fort Venango,* built by the French in 1753, in "the forks of the *Allegheny."* "I prayed the Lord," writes Post, "to blind the French, as he did the enemies of Lot and Elisha, that I might pass unknown." Leaving Venango, Post and his companions turned their horses' heads to the south-west,—struck the *Conequenes-sing* on the 12th of August,—crossed the *Big Beaver,* and next day arrived at *Kaskaskie,* the terminus of their journey and the head-quarters of "The Beaver" and "Shingas," war-chiefs of the Western Delawares. Post was, therefore, the first Moravian west of the Alleghenies. He closes his interesting journal with these words: "Thirty-two days that I lay in the woods, the heavens were my covering, and the dew fell so hard sometimes, that it pricked close to the skin.

beaver-stream. The Indians, however, called the river *Kaskaskie-sipu,* from the town of Kaskaskie on its bank.

BEECH CREEK, (a branch of the Bald Eagle in Centre County), in Delaware, *Schauweminsch-hanne,*[†] i. e., *beech-stream.*

BLACK LICK, (a branch of the Two Licks in Indiana County)—in Delaware, *Neeskahóni,* i. e., a *lick of blackish color.*[‡]

BRUSHY CREEK, (a branch of the Conequenessing in Beaver County)—in Delaware, *Achweek,* i. e., *bushy,* or overgrown with brush.

During this time nothing lay so heavily on my heart as the man who went along with me (*Shamokin Daniel*), for he thwarted me in everything I said or did; not that he did it against me, but against the country on whose business I was sent. When he was with the French he would speak against the English, and when he was with the English he would speak against the French. The Indians observed that he was unreliable, and desired me not to bring him any more to transact business between them and the Province. And it was owing to him, too, that I failed in obtaining an interview with the prisoners. But praise and glory be to the Lamb that was slain, who brought me through a country of dreadful jealousy and mistrust, where the Prince of this world holds rule and government over the children of disobedience. It was my Lord who preserved me amid all difficulties and dangers, and His Holy Spirit directed me. I had no one to commune with but Him; and it was He who brought me from under a thick, heavy and dark cloud into the open air, for which I adore, and praise and worship Him. I know and confess that He, the Lord my God, the same who forgave my sins and washed my heart in his most precious blood, grasped me in his almighty hand and held me safe—and hence I live no longer for myself, but for Him, whose holy will to do is my chiefest pleasure."

The town, or towns of *Kaskaskie* (the *Kaskaskies*), are first mentioned in official records, in Weisser's Journal of his Proceedings at Logstown, fifteen miles below Pittsburg, on the right bank of the Ohio. "To-day (Aug. 29th, 1748), he writes, "my companions went to *Kaskaskie,* a large Indian town about thirty miles off." "Early this morning," (Aug. 17th, 1758) writes Post in his Journal, "the Indians called all the people together to clear the place where they intended to hold the Council, it being in the midst of the town. *Kaskaskie* is divided into *four towns,* each at a distance from the other, and the whole settlement consists of about ninety houses and two hundred able warriors."

Howell's Map notes *Kaskaskie* on the *Little Beaver* or *Mahoning Creek,* now in Lawrence County. Heckewelder crossed the *Big Beaver* in April of 1762, then on his way with Post to the Tuscarawas, (in Stark County, Ohio), the first scene of his missionary labors. Between 1770 and 1773 Moravian Indians under Zeisberger were settled at *Friedensstadt* (Town of Peace), on the West bank of the Big Beaver, in the southern part of Lawrence County, about 15 miles south-east from *Kaskaskie.* Howell's Map notes the site of the Moravian settlement.

† *Schau-we-min-schi,* the red-beech tree.—*Ze.*

‡ *Nees-ki-u,* black. *Nees-ca-lenk,* a negro. *Ma-ho-ny,* a lick.—*Ze.*

BUFFALO CREEK, (a branch of the Allegheny in Armstrong County)—in Delaware, *Sisilie-hánne*, i. e., *buffalo-stream* —a stream whose banks are the resort of the buffalo.

CATASAUQUA, (an affluent of the Lehigh from the North-east in Northampton County), corrupted from *Gattoshácki** signifying, *the earth thirsts*, viz. for rain.

CAT-FISH RUN, (a small stream near the borough of Washington, Washington County). The Delawares called it *Wisaméking*† signifying, *where there is a Cat-fish, where the Cat-fish dwells.*

CATAWISSA, (a branch of the Susquehanna in Columbia County), corrupted from *Gattawisi*,‡ signifying *growing fat.* (*Note.* Probably the Indians who named the place, had shot a deer along the creek in the season when deer fatten.)

CAWANSHANNOCK, (a branch of the Allegheny in Armstrong County), corrupted from *Gawunsch-hánne*, signifying *green-brier* stream.

CHESTER RIVER, (in Delaware County), called in early deeds *Macopanackhan*,§ corrupted from *Meechoppenáckhan*, signifying, *the large potato stream*, i. e., the stream along which large potatoes grow.

CHICKHANSINK, corrupted from *Tshickhánsink*,‖ signifying, *where we were robbed,—the place of the robbery.*

CHICKISALUNGA,¶ (emptying into the Susquehanna from the

---

* *Gat-tos-so-mo*, to thirst. *Hacki*, the earth, the land.—*Zr.* The name is written *Calisuk* and *Caladaqua*, in old deeds. Scull's and Howell's Maps call the stream *Mill Creek*. Scotch-Irish immigrants from Ulster settled on its banks as early as 1737. They were the first white residents within the present limits of Northampton county.

† *Wi-sa-meek*, a cat-fish. Compounded of *we-su*, fat, and *na-mees*, a fish.—*Zr.* "Cat-fish Camp," formerly on the site of the borough of Washington, was so called for the head man of the village, a half-breed, *Cat-fish* by name.

‡ *Wi-sa-heen*, to fatten. *Wi-su*, fat.— *Zr.* *Catawissa*, is regarded by some, as a corruption of *Ganawese*, and as designating the region to which the Conoys retired, on withdrawing from the limits of Lancaster county. See *Conoy* in this paper.

§ *Me-cheek* and *Ma-chee-u*, large. *Hob-be-nac*, potatoes.—*Zr.* The name occurs in an Indian deed executed to William Penn, the 14th day of 5th mo., 1683, "for lands lying between *Manaiunk*, alias Schuylkill and *Macopanackhan*, alias Chester River." The Swedes called the stream *Opland Kill*.

‖ *A-men-tschirch-tin*, to rob, to plunder. *Me-ha-men-tschil*, a robber.—*Zr.*

¶ Shortened into *Chiquis* and *Salunga*, both post-towns in Lancaster County.

North-east in Lancaster County), corrupted from *Chickiswalungo*, *the place of the crawfish*, i. e., where the ground is full of holes bored by the crab or craw-fish.

CHILLISQUAQUE,* (emptying into the Susquehanna from the North-east in Northumberland County), corrupted from *Chilili-suági* signifying, *the place of snow-birds*.

CHINKLACAMOOSE,† now shortened into Moose, (emptying into the Susquehanna from the North-east in Clearfield County, "*the Clear Fields*"), corrupted from *Achtschingi-clamme*, signifying, *it almost joins*, in allusion to a horse-shoe bend in the stream, whose extremities almost unite.

CHOCONUT, (emptying into the Susquehanna in the County of that name) corrupted from the Nanticoke word *Tschochnot*.

CLARION RIVER,‡ (a branch of the Allegheny draining Clarion County), called by the Delawares, *Gawunsch-hánne*, i. e., *brier-stream*,—the stream whose banks are overgrown with the green-brier.

COAQUANNOCK,§ the name by which the site of Philadelphia

---

* Scull's Map locates an Indian village of the same name at the mouth of the creek. "An old Shawano took us in his canoe across the creek at *Zilly-squachne*, for which service I gave him some needles and a pair of shoe strings."—*C. Weiser's Journal to Onondaga.* March, 1737.

† On the site of the county-town of Clearfield, there stood in olden times the village of Chinklacamoose, written *Chinglecamouche*, on Scull's Map. It was the central point of the great "Chinklacamoose Path." Post lodged at this village on his way to the Ohio country in the night of August 2d, 1758. "We arrived," he writes in his Journal, "this night at *Shinglimuee*, where we saw the posts painted red and stuck in the ground, to which the Indians tie their prisoners. It is a disagreeable and melancholy sight to see the means they use to punish flesh and blood."

"July 14th, 1772. We came to the Clearfield creek, so called by the Indians because on its banks there are acres of land that resemble 'clearings;'—the buffalo that resort hither, having destroyed every vestige of undergrowth, and left the face of the country as bare as though it had been cleared by the grub-axe of the pioneer."—*John Ettwein's Journal of the Migration of the Moravian Indians to the Big Beaver.*

‡ Formerly called *Toby's Creek.*

§ "The Proprietary having now returned from Maryland to *Coaquannock*, the place so called by the Indians, where Philadelphia now stands, began to purchase lands of the Indians." *Proud's History of Pennsylvania,* Vol. 1, p. 211. Penn purchased *Coaquannock*, the site of his intended capital, from the three brothers, Andrew, Swen and Ole Swenson, early Swedish settlers on Delaware,—said brothers or other whites having bought the Indian claim, prior to his arrival in the was known to the Indians, is a corruption of *Cawequenáku*, signifying, *the grove of tall pines.*

COCALICO, (a branch of the Conestoga in Lancaster County), corrupted from *Achgookwalico,** (shortened into *Chgokalico*), signifying, *where the snakes collect in dens to pass the winter.* (*Note.* This spot along the Creek was well known to the Indians.)

COCOOSING, (a branch of the Tulpehocken in Berks County), corrupted from *Gokhosing,*† signifying, *where owls are, the place of owls.*

COHOCKSINK, corrupted from *Cuwenhásink,*‡ signifying, *where the pines grow,—where there are pinelands.*

CONESTOGA,§ an Iroquois word.

country in October of 1682. "The Proprietor at his first arrival, finding the Swedes possessed of the most valuable tracts of land on the front of the river, without inquiring into the validity of their titles, but considering them as strangers in an English government, through his known benevolence to mankind was pleased so far to distinguish them by his favors as to confirm to all such as applied to him all their just claims, to the great disappointment of those English adventurers who embarked with him and hazarded their lives and fortunes in the commendable design of peopling this colony; or where it was found necessary to apply any of those claims to other purposes, he was pleased to make very ample compensation for them; a pregnant instance of which, is his grant of 600 acres of land to the Swensons in lieu of a very slender claim they had to about half that quantity in the place where it was judged most convenient this city should be built."—*Report of Petition of the Swedes*, 1721. *Penn'a Archives, Vol. 1, p. 172.*

* *Ach-gook*, a snake. *Woa-lac*, a hole. *Suck-ack-gook*, a black snake—*M'hi-uch-gook*, a water-snake;—*As-gash-ach-gook*, a green snake;—*Mach-go-u-ach-gook*, a copper-snake.—*Zr.*

Heckewelder, in his Narrative, states that the Western Indians, who were signally defeated by Gen. Wayne at the Rapids of the Miami in August of 1794, called him *Suckachgook*, because of the caution and cunning he displayed in his movements throughout the campaign.

† *Gok-hoos*, an owl, *Gok-ho-til*, an owlet.—*Zr.* *Ink*, the local suffix *at*, or, *where.* On Dec. 28, 1742, Zinzendorf preached in a farm-house on the Cocoosing.

‡ *Cu-we*, a pine. *Ha-cki*, land.—*Zr.* *Ink*, the local suffix *at*, or *where.*

§ On the flats east of Turkey Hill at the mouth of the Conestoga in Manor Township, dwelt the small tribe of the Conestogas, whom Wm. Penn is said to have visited in their town, and to retain whose friendship despite the machinations of French emissaries, his Lieut. Governors exercised constant precaution. Hence James Logan repaired to Conestoga in 1705, Gov. Evans in 1707, Gov. Gookin in 1710, Gov. Keith in 1717 and Gov. Gordon in 1728. *Tagodalessa*, or *Civility*, a chief of this tribe is often named in the records of those days. It was he who wrote that touching letter in which grief for the loss of a beloved child appears in almost every line. "The late death of my child causes so much trouble

CONEWANGO, (a branch of the Allegheny in Warren County), corrupted from *Guneúnga,** signifying, *they have been gone a long time, they stay a long time.*

CONEWANTA, (emptying into the Susquehanna in the County of that name) corrupted from *Guneúnga,* signifying, *they stay long time.*

CONNEAUT, (a branch of French Creek in Crawford County), corrupted from *Gunniati,* signifying, *it is a long time since he or they are gone.*

CONOCOCHEAGUE,† (a branch of the Potomac draining Franklin County), corrupted from *Guneukitschik,* signifying, *indeed a long way!* a name expressive of impatience manifested by a company of Indians traveling along the stream.

CONODOGWINET, (a branch of the Susquehanna draining Cumberland County), corrupted from *Gunnipduckhánnet,‡* signifying, *for a long way nothing but bends.*

CONONODAW, (one of the head branches of the Allegheny in McKean County), corrupted from *Gunniáda,* signifying, *he tarries long.* (*Note.* A name expressive of the impatience of some In-

and sorrow at this time, it puts all other thoughts out of my mind—my grief and sorrow overpower me—my eyes are full of tears for the sake of my child. My trouble is so great at this time that it puts all other thoughts out of my mind, so that I do nothing but cry every day. When my grief and sorrow are a little over, you shall hear from us, even if I do not come myself!" The Conestogas remained on their old seats long after the other Indians on the Susquehanna had been crowded by the advance of civilization beyond Shamokin, and it was upward of sixty years after William Penn had been at their town, and full twenty-five after *Tagodalessa* has ceased grieving for his child, that they were barbarously exterminated to a man, by the Scotch-Irish partisans of Paxton.

* *Gu-ne u,* long. *Gu-nax-u,* it is long. *Gu-ni,* a long while. *Gu-na ge-u,* he stays long —*Zr.*

† *Gu-ne u,* long. *Hi-tschi-wi,* indeed.—*Zr.* The valley of the Conococheague was explored and settled about 1730, by Scotch-Irish pioneers, among whom were three brothers, by the name of Chambers. The site of Chambersburg at the confluence of Falling Spring and the Conococheague was built on by Joseph Chambers. The "Conococheague Settlement" suffered much from the Indians, after Braddock's defeat in 1755. Moravian itinerants visited the lower valley in Maryland, as early at 1748.

‡ *Gu-ne-u,* long. *P'tuk hanne,* a bend in a river.—*Zr.* An inspection of the map will show the appropriate application of this euphonious Indian name. When John Harris settled on Paxton Creek, (see Paxton in this register) there were Shawanese planting at the mouth of the Conodogwinet, on the right bank of the Susquehanna.

dians, when halting along the creek to await the return of one of their companions.)

CONOQUENESSING, (a branch of the Allegheny, draining Butler County), corrupted from *Gunachquenésink,** signifying, *for a long way straight.*

COXOY,† (a small creek emptying into the Susquehanna in Lancaster County), corrupted from *Guncu,* signifying, *long.*

* *Gu-ne-u,* long. *Schu-chuch-ge-u,* straight.—*Ze.*

† This creek perpetuates the name of the *Conoy, Ganawese* or *Piscatawa* Indians, who in 1700 entered the Province from the South, and settled "near the head of *Potomok.*" For upwards of 40 years, we find their deputies participating in conferences held with Wm. Penn, or with the Proprietaries' Governors at Philadelphia, or on the Susquehanna. In 1705, (at which time they were reduced by sickness to a small number) they requested permission of Gov. Evans, through *Manangy,* "the Indian Chief on Schuylkill," to settle among the Schuylkill Indians near *Tulpehocken.* Instead, however, they planted *some miles above Conestoga,* at *Connejahera.* Their village here was called *Dekanouga,* and the Governor states it to have been *nine miles distant from Pequea.* In 1719, the Conoy Town, we learn, was a halting-point for warriors of the Five Nations, as they returned north from marauds against the Catawbas of Virginia and the Carolinas. In June of 1733 the *Conoys* or *Ganawese* "living between Paxton and Conestoga," sent a messenger to Shikellimy of Shamokin, (for being tributaries of the Six Nations they looked to Shikellimy for counsel) to inform him of intelligence come to them, to the effect that the Governor of Virginia was about to send a party of armed men to cut them off for a murder committed within his jurisdiction, and charged to them. In May of 1743, Gov. Thomas laid before the Board the following letter written by Thomas Cookson, of Lancaster, at the instance of the Conoy Indians. "The Indians of the *Conoytown on the east side of Susquehanna,* in April last, sent me a message, signifying their having something to communicate to your Honor, and desired me to be at home on the 11th of the same month, on which day they came down to the number of fourteen. Having invited them into the house, *Old Sack,* their chief, spoke to the following purpose: We desire you to acquaint our brother the Governor, that our forefathers came from *Piscatua* to an island in Potomock, and from there down to Philadelphia in old Proprietor Penn's time (May 1701) in order to show their friendship to the Proprietor;—that after their return they brought down all their brothers from Potomock to *Conejohela,* on the east side of Susquehanna, and built a town there,—that the Six Nations had told them there was land enough, they might choose their place of settlement any where about Susquehanna,—that accordingly they thought fit to remove higher up that river to the Conoytown where they now live; and on their first settling there, the Indians of the Six Nations came down and made their fire, and all the great men declared the fire of their kindling to be in token of their approbation of the settlement; but that now the land all around them being settled by white people, their hunting is spoiled, and they have been long advised by the Six Nations to leave their place and go higher up the river, either at the mouth of *Conedoguinet* or of *Ju-*

COSHECTON, (a branch of the Susquehanna in the County of that name) corrupted from *Gischiechton*,* signifying, *finished, complete.*

COWANESQUE, (a branch of the Tioga in Tioga County), corrupted from *Gawunshesque*, signifying *overgrown with briers, briery.*

CROOKED CREEK, (emptying into the Allegheny from the Southeast in Armstrong County),—in Delaware, *Woak-hánne*,† i. e., *crooked stream*, the streams with large bends.

CROSS CREEK, (a branch of the Ohio, heading in Washington County.). A creek bearing the same name empties into the Ohio from the West. The two are called the Cross Creeks—in Delaware, *Wewuntschi saquick*, words signifying, *two streams flowing into a river at the same point from opposite directions.*

DELAWARE RIVER,‡ called by the Delawares *Lenape-wihittuck*, i. e., *the river of the Lenape.* Also *Kit-hánne*, (in Minsi Delaware *Gicht-hánne*) signifying, the *main stream* in its region of country.

DUCK CREEK, (in Delaware) called in early Indian deeds *Quing Quingus*,§ corrupted from *Quiquingus*, the Delaware name for the *mallard*, or common *wild duck.*

ELK CREEK, (emptying into the Susquehanna from the South, in Lycoming County),—in Delaware *Mos-hánne* or *Moos-hánne*,‖ i. e., *Elk-stream.*

---

niuda, or to *Shamokin.*" In August of 1744, Shikellimy reported to the Governor, that "the Conoy Indians having moved higher up to be nearer us. we desire to inform the Governor of it, and on their behalf give this string of wampum." In 1749 the Conoys were residing "among other Indian nations at Juniata." *Conniack*, represented the Conoys, in a private conference held by the Proprietaries' agents with the chief of the United Nations, at the house of Adam Yohe in Easton, Oct. 24, 1758. Bainbridge, at the mouth of the Conoy in Conoy township, is said to occupy the site of the last settlement of the Ganawese in Lancaster county.

* *Gi-schieck-en*, finished, done.—*Zr.*

† *Woak-tschin-ni*, to bend. *Woak-tsche-u*, crooked.—*Zr.*

‡ *Len-na-pe*, an Indian. *Len-na-pe-wak*, Indians.—*Zr.* The Dutch who were the first Europeans to sail up the Delaware named it in contradistinction from the North River, *Zuydt* or *South River.* It takes its present name from Lord De la Ware, Governor of Virginia, who passed the Capes in 1610.—*Kik-hi-can* and *Kik-hit-tuk*, a large river. *Kid-han nünk*, in, or, at the large or main river.—*Zr.*

§ *Qui-quin-gus*, large ducks.—*Zr.* This name occurs in a deed executed to Wm. Penn, by certain Indian kings. Sachemakers (*Sa-ki-ma*, chief, king.—*Zr.*) at New Castle, the 2d day of 8 mo. 1685, for lands "from *Quing Quin-gus*, called Duck Creek unto Upland, called Chester Creek, all along by the west side of Delaware River, and so between the said Creeks backwards, as far as a man can ride in two days with a horse."

‖ *Moos*, a cow. *Moo-sak*, cattle.—*Zr.*

ELK LICK, (one of the sources of the Sinnemahoning in Potter County),—in Delaware, *Mosi-mahóni.*

EQUINUNK, (emtying into the Delaware from the south-west in Wayne County.) The word is Delaware, and signifies, *where articles of clothing were distributed.*

FISHING CREEK, (emptying into the Bald Eagle from the South, in Clinton County,) in Delaware, *Namees-hánne,*[*] i. e., *fish-stream.*

HOCKENDAUQUA, (emptying into the Lehigh from the North-east in Northampton County), corrupted from *Hackiundochwe,*[†] signifying, *searching for land.* (Note. Probably some whites were observed by the Indians surveying or prospecting along this stream.)

HOPPENY CREEK, (emptying into the Susquehanna from the West, in Wyoming County), corrupted from *Hobbenisink,*[‡] signifying, *where there are wild potatoes.*

JUNIATA,[§] an Iroquois word. The Delawares say *Juchniáda,* or *Chuchniada.* (Note. The Iroquois had a path leading to a Shawanese town on the Raystown branch of the Juniata, situated, I am told on the site of Bedford.)

---

[*] *Na-mees,* a fish. *Na-me-sac,* fishes. *Na-me-si-pook,* it tastes fishy.—*Zr.*

[†] *Ha-cki,* land. *Un-dooch-wen,* to come for some purpose.—*Zr.* Surveyor-General Eastburn's Map of the Forks of Delaware, drawn in 1740, notes three surveys on the Hockendauqua, one of 1800 acres, another of 1426 acres, marked *William Allen,* and a third of 1500 acres, marked *John Page.* These surveys were made prior to the walk of a day and a half in Sept. of 1737. *Lappawinzor* (whose portrait was presented to the Historical Society of Pennsylvania, by the late Granville Penn), at that time king of Hockendauqua, witnessed the walk in part, and expressed his dissatisfaction at the walkers in the memorable words—"No sit down to smoke—no shoot a squirrel; but lun, lun, lun all day long!" His village lay between Howell's grist-mill and the mouth of the Creek. Near it the tired walkers passed the night of the 19th and 20th of September, on the completion of a twelve hours' walk, bivouacking before a blazing fire, while the Indians in the village below prolonged a cantico till into the hours of the early morning.

[†] *Hobbenac,* wild potatoes.—*Zr.*

[‡] Written also *Neokooniady, Choniata* and *Chiniatta.* "Shikellimy then asked the Proprietor (Thos. Penn) whether he had heard of a letter which he and Sassoonan (Allummapees) had sent to John Harris to desire him to desist from making a plantation at the mouth of *Choniata,* where Harris had built a house and is clearing fields. They were told that Harris had only built the house for carrying on his trade,—that his plantation at Paxton is his place of dwelling, and it is not to be supposed he will remove from thence. Shikellimy said he had no ill will to John Harris, it not being his custom to bear any man ill will, but he is afraid that the warriors of the Six Nations when they pass that way may take it

KENJUA, (a branch of the Allegheny, heading in McKean County), corrupted from *Kéntschuak*, signifying, *they gobble.* (*Note.* The creek was evidently a resort of wild turkeys, the name it bears alluding to the *gobbling* with which the turkey-cock responds to the call of his mate.)

KIGISCHGOTAM, corrupted from *Kikischcotam*,* Delaware for *katy-did.*

KIKITSCHIMUS, (Duck Creek) corrupted from *Kikitschimus*,† Delaware for *wood* or *tree-duck.*

KISHICOQUILLAS,‡ (emptying into the Juniata from the North, in Mifflin County), corrupted from *Gischichgakwalis*, signifying, *the snakes are already in their dens;* compounded of *gischi*, already —*achgook*, snakes—and *walieu*, in dens.

KISKIMINETAS or Conemaugh, (a branch of the Allegheny dividing Armstrong and Indiana Counties from Westmoreland), corrupted from *Gieschgumanito*,§ signifying, *make daylight!* (*Note.*

---

ill to see a settlement made on lands which they have always desired to be kept free." *Minutes of Prov. Council, June* 19, 1733.

"Bro. Onas! The Dutchman on *Scokooniady* claims a right to the land merely because he gave a little victuals to our warriors, who stand very often in need of it. This string of wampum serves to take the Dutchman by the arm and to throw him over the big mountain within your borders. We have given the River *Scokooniady* for a hunting-place to our cousins the Delawares, and our brothers the Shawanese, and we ourselves hunt there sometimes. We therefore desire you will immediately by force remove all those that live on the river of *Scokooniady*." *Council of Onondaga to Gov. Thomas, April* 9, 1743.

The Shawanese town alluded to in Mr. Heckewelder's note, may have been the "Shawanese Cabins," noted on Scull's Map, and situate about 8 miles west of Raystown, on the Raystown branch of the Juniata.

* *Ki-gisch-go-tum*, green grasshoppers.—*Zr.*

† *Gi-gi-tschi-mu-is*, a summer-duck.—*Zr.*

‡ In an enumeration of Indians residing within the Province, furnished to Government by Jonah Davenport and James Letort, traders, in October of 1731, *Ohesson* is mentioned as an Indian town on *Choniata*, 60 miles from Susquehanna, inhabited by 20 families of Shawanese, numbering 60 men, and *Kissikahquilas*, their chief.

Conrad Weisser writes from Aughwick, Sept. 3, 1754, as follows: "I also condoled with the Indians in the name of this Government over the death of the Shawanese chief, who died at Capt. McKee's in Paxton, last month. His name was *Kissakoochquilla*.

§ *Gisch-gu*, day. *Gisch-que*, to-day. *Gi-scha-pan*, it is day-break. *Ma-ni-toon*, to make.—*Zr.* "On Conemaugh Creek there are three Shawanese towns, 45 families, 200 men, and *Okowela* their chief." *Report of Jonah Davenport and*

4

Probably the word of command given by a warrior to his comrades at night, to break up camp and resume the journey or warpath.)

KITTANNING,* (the County-seat of Armstrong), corrupted from *Kit-hánne*, in Minsi Delaware, *Gicht-hánne*, signifying, *the main stream*, i. e., in its region of country.

LACKAMISSA, (corrupted from *Legau-miksa*,† signifying, *sandy soil.*

LACKAWANNOCK, (emptying into the Susquehanna from the North-east in Luzerne County,) corrupted from *Lechauwáh-han-nek*,‡ or *Lechau-hánnek*, signifying, *the forks of a stream.*

LACKAWAXEN, (a branch of the Delaware in Wayne and Pike Counties), corrupted from *Lechauwésink*, signifying, *where the roads part*—at the forks of the road.§

LEHIGH RIVER, called by the Delawares *Lechauwécki*, *Lechau-wicchink*, or *Lechauwékink*,‖ signifying, *where there are forks.* This

---

James Letort, Oct. 29, 1731. *"Aug. 25, 1748. Crossed Kiskeminetas Creek*, and came to Ohio, that day traveling 20 miles."—*Weisser's Journal to Logstown.*

* On the alluvial flat on the left bank of the Alleghany, where Kittanning was laid out in 1804, there stood in Colonial times an Indian village of the same name, and through it passed a great trail called the "*Kittaning Path*," by which the Indians of the West communicated with those of the Susquehanna country. Scull's Map calls it "the Ohio Path." In August of 1756, Col. John Armstrong fitted out an expedition at Fort Shirley, and attacked and burned the 30 houses which composed the Indian town of Kittaning "on Ohio," then the head-quarters of the Delaware war-chief, Capt. Jacobs.

† *Le-kau*, sand.—*Zr.*

‡ *L'chau-hanne*, the fork of a river or stream.—*Zr.*

§ The head-line of the so-called "walking purchase," run by Surveyor General Eastburn at right angles to the line of the walk, extended from the "five chestnut-oaks cut with the Proprietaries' initials and the year 1737, at the end of the day's and a half walk through a mountainous barren country abounding in pines" to a tree *near the mouth of the Lackawaxen*, on Delaware, marked with the letter P.

‖ *Le-chau-wook*, a fork. *L'chau-wa-quot*, a sapling with a fork. *L'chau-wic-chen*, the fork of a road. *L'chau-henne-wall*, the forks of streams. *Lal-chau wu lin-scha-ja*, the forks of the fingers. *Lal-chau nch-si-ta-ja*, the forks of the toes.—*Zr.* The Lehigh River is noticed in records of the Province as early as 1701. On the 21st of March of that year, the Proprietary and Governor informed the Council "that a certain young Swede arriving from *Lechay*, brought intelligence that on 5th day last some young men going out a hunting at that place, heard the frequent report of fire-arms, which made them suspect that the Senecas were coming down among them." "*March* 31, 1701. The Proprietary and Governor acquainted the Board that despite a law prohibiting all persons to trade with the Indians in this name was given to the River, because through it struck an'Indian path or thoroughfare coming from the lower parts of the Delaware country, which thoroughfare, on the left bank of the River, *forked off into various trails*, leading North and West. The word *Lechauwékink*, was shortened into *Lecha*, the name still in use among the descendants of German settlers,—of which abbreviation *Lehigh* is a corruption.

Lechau-hánne, literally a *forked stream*, is the word also applied by the Delawares to the angle or wedge of land lying between the confluence of two streams. *The forks*, most frequently alluded to in early records of Provincial Pennsylvania, are those of the Delaware and its *West Branch* or Lehigh—called the *Forks of the Delaware*.

Lechauwítank, the place at or within the forks, was the name given by the Delawares to the site of Easton, and then to the town.

Province, but such as dwell and reside therein, and have a license from the Governor,—John Hans Stiehlman, said to live in Maryland, and to have no such license, followed a close trade with the Indians of this Province, not only at Conestoga, but had been endeavoring to settle a trade with those at *Lechay*, or ye *Forks of Delaware*, to the great prejudice of the trade of this Province, for which reason the Governor had seized such of his goods as were going to *Lechay*." To John Hans, the Governor thereupon wrote ,as follows: "Thy present management of the Indian trade is directly contrary to our laws. I have therefore stopped thy goods intended for *Lechay*, till according to thy frequent engagements thou come hither thyself and give further satisfaction than thou hast yet done, to

"Thy friend, WILLIAM PENN."

"*July* 25, 1701. The Proprietary and Governor ordered that Menangy, Indian chief on Schuylkill, *Oppemenyhook, Chief on Lechay*, and Indian Harry of Conestoga be sent for to consult with about passing a law to prohibit all use of rum to the Indians of their nations."

"Last week thy son, Judge Mompesson, and myself went to Pennsbury to meet one hundred Indians, of which nine are kings. *Oppewanumhook* (Oppemenyhook?) the chief, with his neighbors, who came hither to congratulate thy son's arrival, presented nine belts of wampum for a ratification of peace, and had returns accordingly."

James Logan to William Penn, Philadelphia, 14th 1 month, 1710.
Memoirs of the Hist'l Society of Penn'a, Vol. IX.

The " Indian Ford," alluded to above, crossed the Lehigh at the head of the island opposite the works of the " Bethlehem Iron Company," and was included in the purchase of 500 acres made by the Moravians of Abraham Taylor in February of 1756. When, in 1745, a road was laid out from the grist-mill at Bethlehem, to the terminus of the King's Road from Philadelphia at Irish's stone quarry, the " Indian Ford" was included in the survey.

LICKING CREEK, (a branch of the Potomac heading in Bedford County). In Delaware, *Mahonink*, signifying, *where there is a lick*.

LITTLE BEAVER, (a branch of the Ohio in Beaver County). In Delaware, *Tank-amochk-hánne*, i. e., *little beaver-stream*.

LITTLE BRIER, (in Jefferson County?) In Delaware, *Tanga-wunsch-hánne* i. e., *little brier stream*.

LITTLE CONEMAUGH, (a branch of the Conemaugh or Kiskiminetas in Cambria County). The Delawares called it *Gunamóchki*,* *the little otter*.

LITTLE MOSHANNON, (a branch of the Moshannon in Centre County). In Delaware *Tankimoos-hánne*, i. e., *little elk stream*.

LITTLE SCHUYLKILL, Beaver, or Tamaque Creek, (a branch of the Schuylkill in Schuylkill County). In Delaware, *tamaque-hánne*, i. e., *beaver stream,*—a stream across which the beaver throws a dam and builds his lodge.

LOYALHANNA,† (a branch of the Conemaugh or Kiskiminetas in Westmoreland County), corrupted from *Laweel-hánne*, signifying, *the middle stream*.

LOYALSOCK,‡ (a branch of the Susquehanna in Lycoming County), corrupted from *Lawi-saquick*, signifying the *middle creek*, i. e., a creek flowing between two others.

LYCOMING,§ (a branch of the Susquehanna in Lycoming County), corrupted from *Legaui-hánne*, signifying *sandy stream*. The Delawares called it invariably by this name.

MACUNGY, (a township in Lehigh County) corrupted from *Machk-ánschi*,|| signifying, *the feeding place of bears*.

---

* *Gun-na moochk*, an otter,—*Zr.* Compounded of *gu-ne-u* long and *a-moochk* a beaver.

† *Le la-wi*, the middle. *Lawi-lo-wan*, mid-winter. *La-wit-pi-cat*, mid-night. *La-wu-linsch-gan*, the middle finger. *La-wu-linsch*, the middle or palm of the hand.—*Zr.*

‡ Count Zinzendorf was at the Indian town of *Ots-ton-wa-kin*, at the mouth of the Loyalsock, in October of 1742, said town at that time being the residence of Madame Montour. (See Memorials of the Moravian Church, Vol. 1, p. 80, for the Count's narrative.)

§ Written Lycaumick on Scull's Map. *French Margaret's Town*, stood on the right bank of the creek, near its outlet.

|| *Machk*, a bear. *Mach-qui-ge-u*, plenty of bears. *Mach-quik*, there are bears plenty.—*Zr.* The region of country drained by the Little Lehigh and its tributaries (since 1812 in Lehigh County) embracing the townships of Upper and Lower Macungy and Salsburg, was called *Macaunsic* and *Macquenusic* prior to 1735, and

MEECH-HÁNNE,|| (signifying, *the main stream;* a name applied to the *largest* of several affluent streams, prior to their confluence. This was the name given by the Delawares to the main branch of the Lehigh, (between Luzerne and Monroe), it being larger than either the *Toby-hanna,* or the *Tunk-hanna,* its other sources.

MECHEEK-MENÁTEY,* i. e., *the Great Island,* the name in use among the Delawares.

MAHANOY,† (a branch of the Susquehanna in Northumberland County), corrupted from *mahoni, a lick.*

MAHANTANGO,‡ (a branch of the Susquehanna between Dauphin and Northumberland Counties), corrupted from *Mohantango,* signifying, *where we had plenty of meat to eat.*

MAHONING,§ (a branch of the Lehigh, heading west in Carbon County), corrupted from *Mahonink,* signifying, *where there is a lick, at the lick. Mahoni* is Delaware for *a lick, mahonittly* signifies, *a diminutive lick,* and *mahon-hánne, a stream flowing from or near a lick.*

---

was already then in part well settled by German immigrants. In March of that year, "sundry of the inhabitants of Bucks living near and at *Macaunsie,* in a petition to Gov. Gordon, set forth the great necessity of a public road from their settlements to *Goshen-hoppen,*" a return of which road was made in January of 1736. The Moravians labored in the Gospel among the Germans of Macungy as early as 1742, in July of which year Gottlieb Pezold, of Bethlehem, occupied that field. It was one of the few outside of their own settlements in which they effected a permanent footing. In 1747 they organized a congregation among the settlers near the South Mountain, five miles South-west from Allentown, and also established a school, which was in operation until 1754. About this time Salsburg township was erected. In 1761 the Moravian village within its bounds was named *Emmaus,* now a station on the East Penn R. R.

|| *Me-check* and *Mach-we-u,* great, large. *Meech-gi-lük,* the large one. *Meech-han-ne,* a large stream.—*Zr.*

* *Me-na-tey,* and *Me-na-ten,* an island.—*Zr.* This island lies in the West Branch of the Susquehanna, in that long stretch of the river, called *Quenischa-schachki,* not far from Dunnstown, Lycoming County. It was a favorite resort of the Indians and lay on one of the great thoroughfares of the Delaware country.

† Zinzendorf, on his way to Shamokin in Sept. of 1742, named the Mahanoy *Leimbach's Creek,* for Henry Leimbach, of Oley, one of his fellow-travelers.

‡ The Count on the same journey named the Mahantango, *Benigna's Creek,* in honor of his daughter.

§ Compounded of *Mahoni,* a lick, and *ink* or *ing,* the local suffix. This name was a very common one for rivers and places in the Delaware country, along which or where the surface of the ground was covered with saline deposit or efflorescence, provincially called "*licks*" from the fact of deer and elk frequenting them and *licking* the saltish earth.

MAKERISK-KITTON.* This name, written also *Makeusk-kitton*, *Makerisk-hickon* and *Makeerick-kitton* in early Indian deeds, denotes, I am inclined to believe, a spot either on the bank, or in the bed of the Delaware;—which conjecture I base on the termination *kitton*, evidently intended for *kit-hánne* or *gicht-hanne*, signifying *the main stream*.

MANAHAN, (a branch of the Yellow Breeches in York County), corrupted from *menéhund*,† signifying *where liquor had been drunk*.

MANALTIN, corrupted from *menaltink*, signifying, *where we drank liquor to excess*.

MANATAWNY,‡ (a branch of the Schuylkill in Berks County), corrupted from *menháttunink*, signifying, *where we drank liquor*.

MANAYUNK,§ corrupted from *mene-iunk*, signifying, *where we go to drink—our place of drinking liquor*.

---

* The name occurs in the deed executed by the Indians to Wm. Markham, (Penn's deputy,) on the 15th July, 1782, (the oldest Indian deed on record), in which indenture the tract of land conveyed to the Proprietor is described as "lying in the Province of Pennsylvania, beginning at a certain white oak on the land now in the tenure of John Wood, and by him called the Gray Stones over against the falls of Delaware River, and so from thence up by the River's side to a corner marked spruce-tree with the letter P, at the foot of a mountain, and from the said corner marked spruce-tree along by the ledge or foot of the mountains, west north-west to a corner white-oak marked with the letter P, standing by the Indian path that leads to an Indian town called *Playwickey*, and near the head of a creek called *Towsissinock*, and from thence westward to the Creek called *Neshamony's Creek*, and along by the said *Neshamony's Creek* unto the river Delaware, alias, *Makerisk-hickon*, and so bounded by the said *main river*, to the said first-mentioned white-oak in John Wood's land." This purchase situate within the great bend of the Delaware, and between the falls opposite Trenton and the Neshaminy, was made by Markham for Penn's private use, and became the seat of the *Manor of Pennsbury*.

The curious instrument from which the above recital of boundaries was taken is in the possession of the Historical Society of Pennsylvania.

† *Me-nee-ton*, to spend in drinking. *Me-neel*, drink. *Mee-neet*, a drinkard. *Me-ne-wou-can*, drinking.—*Zr.*

‡ Manatawny is mentioned in official records as early as July of 1707. In May of 1728 it was the scene of a collision between the settlers and some Shawanese who had come down from *Pechoqualin* armed, and with a Spanish Indian, as it was thought, for their Captain. Many of the back inhabitants in consequence quitted their houses, being under apprehension of numbers of foreign Indians, Twightwees or Flatheads, coming to attack them, and several Palatine families gathered together in a mill near New Hanover, there to defend themselves.

§ Occurs in the deed cited under Chester River, in this register.

MASGEEK-HÁNNE,* *swamp-stream*, the name given by the Delawares to a run flowing through the swamp of the Broad Mountain in Monroe County.

MAUCH CHUNK, corrupted from *machk-tschunk*,† signifying *bear-mountain*, or strictly, *where there is a mountain, the resort of bears*.

MAXATAWNY,‡ (a branch of Saucon Creek in Berks County), corrupted from *machksit-hánne*, signifying *bear's path stream*,—the stream along which bears have beaten a path.

MENIOLOGAMEKA,§ the name of an Indian village on the *Achquoanschicóla*, at the northern base of the Blue Mountain, near Smith's Gap.

MESHOPPEN, (emptying into the Susquehanna from the North in Wyoming County), corrupted from *maschápi*,‖ signifying, *glass-beads*, a name given by the Indians to commemorate a distribution of such trinkets, made somewhere on the bank of the stream.

MINISINK, corrupted from *Mins-ink* or *Miníssink*, signifying, *where there are Minsies*, i. e., the home or country of the Minsies.¶

---

* *Mas-keek*, a swamp. *Mas-ke-kunk*, in the swamp.— *Zr.*

† *Machk*, a bear. *Wach-tschu*, a mountain. *Wachtschuwall*, mountains. *Wach-tschunk*, on the mountain.—*Zr.*

‡ Also the name of a township in Berks, in which, at the house of Jacob De Levan, a French Huguenot, Zinzendorf preached in 1742. Scull's Map notes Delevan on the road from Easton to Reading, about six miles West of Mertztown.

§ See Memorials of the Moravian Church, Vol. 1, p. 35. Heckewelder in his Narrative states that the word implies *a rich spot of ground surrounded by barren lands.*

‖ *Ma-scha-pi*, corals, beads. *Woop-a-schapi-all*, white beads.—*Zr.*

¶ Early records assign this division of the Lenape, to the North-eastern wilds of the Province, within the country which is called on old maps "the land abounding in the sugar tree." The upper valley of the Delaware, however, was pre-eminently the home of the Minsies, (the historic Minsinks,) where they built their towns, planted their corn and kindled their council fires, and whence they set out on the hunt or on the war-path. The *Minsies, Monseys*, or *Muncys*, were the most warlike of their people, and proverbially impatient of the white man's presence in the Indian country. The murder of one Wright at John Burt's house in Snaketown, in Sept. of 1727, was the act of *Minsies*, and subjects we are told of Kindassowa, who resided "at the Forks of the Susquehanna above Mechayomy." The following notice of the physical peculiarities and traits of these mountaineers, is copied from a paper, in the hand-writing of Mr. Heckewelder. "According to my observation and judgment of Indian tribes, the Minsies have a peculiarity which signalises them from other nations or tribes; and I have seldom failed in pointing them out among a crowd, where they, Delawares and Mohicans were to-

MOHULBUCTEETAM, now Mahoning Creek, (a branch of the
Allegheny in Armstrong County), corrupted from *Mochoolpakiton*,*
signifying, *where canoes are abandoned*, i. e., the head of navigation.

MONOCASY, (a branch of the Lehigh in Northampton County),
corrupted from *Menágassi*, or *Menakessi*, signifying, *a stream with
several large bends*.†

MONODY, (a branch of the Swatara in Dauphin County), corrupted from *Menatey*, signifying, *an island*.

MONONGAHELA, corrupted from *Menaungehilla*, a word imply-
ing *high banks or bluffs, breaking off and falling down at places*.

MOSELEM, (a branch of Maiden Creek in Berks County), corrupted from *Meschilameck-hánne*,‡ signifying *trout stream*.

MOSHANNON, (emptying into the Susquehanna from the South-
west, between Clearfield and Centre Counties), corrupted from
Mooshánne, i. e., *elk stream*.

MUNCY CREEK,§ (an affluent of the Susquehanna in Lycoming

---

gether. The principal distinguishing marks with me, are—robust or strong-boned,
broad faces, somewhat surly countenances, greater head of hair and this growing
low down on their foreheads, short, round-like nose, thick lips seldom closed, or
rather having their mouths generally somewhat open, which, as I am inclined to
believe, may be owing in some measure to an awkward custom of this people, who,
instead of pointing to a thing or object with their hands or fingers, as other Indians do, generally draw out their mouths or lips in the desired direction. They
are averse to manners, prone to mischief and friends of war. Their natural com-
plexion is dark, more so than any Indians I have yet seen, but being within these
twenty last years much mixed by intermarriages with other tribes, their color has
become lighter or fairer."

" From the Falls of Delaware River the Indians go in canoes up the said river
to an Indian town called Minisinks, which is accounted from the Falls about 80
miles; but this they perform by great labor in setting up against the stream. I
have been informed that about Minisinks by the river-side, both in New Jersey
and Pennsylvania are great quantities of exceeding rich open land which is occa-
sioned by washing down of the leaves and soil in great rains from the mountains."
A True Account of Pennsylvania and New Jersey, by Thomas Budd, 1685.

The settlement of "the Minisinks" by whites from Esopus prior to the purchase
of the Indian claim, (ostensibly consummated by the "one and a half day's walk,"
in the autumn of 1737) was one of the grievances that alienated the Delawares
from the English, and provoked the war of 1755.

* *A-mo-chool*, a canoe. *Pa-ki-ton*, to throw away.—*Zr*.

† *Menagachsink*, was the name given by the Delawares to the site of Bethlehem
at the mouth of the Monakasy.

‡ *Me-schi-la-meek*, a trout. *Ma-schi-la-me-quak*, trouts.—*Zr*.

§ Called *Ocochpocheny*, on Scull's Map. Zinzendorf and his companions were

County), corrupted from *Mins-ink,* signifying, *where there are Minsies.*

NESCOPEC, (emptying into the Susquehanna from the East in Luzerne County), corrupted from *Neskchoppeek,** signifying *black, deep and still water.*

NESHAMINY, (a branch of the Delaware in Bucks County), corrupted from *Niwcham-hánne,†* signifying *a double stream,* i. e., a stream formed by the confluence of two branches.

NESHANNOCK, (emptying into the Beaver from the North in Lawrence County), corrupted from *Nishannok,* signifying, *both streams, two adjoining streams.*

NESQUEHONING, (emptying into the Lehigh from the West, in Carbon County), corrupted from *Neska-honi,* signifying, a *black lick.*

NIPPENOSE, (draining Nippenose Bottom, and emptying into the Susquehanna from the South, in Lycoming County), corrupted from *Nipeno-wi,‡* signifying, *like the summer,* a name indicating a warm and genial situation.

---

the first Moravians to cross Muncy Creek. It was in September of 1742. "In the afternoon of Sunday, Aug. 26, 1753, we launched our canoe and paddled up the river. Four miles above Shamokin we came to *Logan's* place. The few Indians who reside here informed us that he had gone to the Seneca country. In one of the cabins there lay a Shawano dying of small-pox. The poor fellow had just returned with two *Tudelars* from an unsuccessful expedition against the Catawbas, in which the captain of his company, an Oneida, and four other comrades lost their lives. On the 27th we arrived at *John Shıkellimy's* hunting-lodge (*quaere,* at the mouth of Warrior's Run ?). The Shawanese here gave us a friendly reception, supplying us also with bear's meat, in return for which Bro. Grubé made the children a present of dried apples. After dinner we came to the mouth of *Muncy Creek,* 40 *miles above Shamokin.* As the Susquehanna was high and the current rapid, we left our canoe in care of an Indian acquaintance, shouldered our packs, and keeping along the bank of the river, arrived at *Otstonwakin* in the evening.—*Journal of Mack and Grubé from Bethlehem to Quenischaschachki.*

* *Neesk-i-u,* black. *Tup-peek,* a spring, a well.—*Zr.*

† *Nis-chi,* two. *Ni-schi-nach-ke,* twenty. *Ni-sche-cat,* double.—*Zr.* The name occurs in the deed of July 1682, cited under *Makerısk-kitton.* When in July of 1742, Zinzendorf inaugurated a work of home-missions in the rural districts of the Province, he sent John Okely, of Bethlehem, to preach to the English settlers on the Neshaminy. His appointments were probably at Hartsville, a small village on the Willow Grove Turnpike, about six miles south from Doylestown, not far from the Neshaminy Church and the "Log College," both of which were in charge of the Rev. William Tennent.

‡ *Ni-pen,* summer. *Ni-pin-ke,* in the summer. *Ni pe-na-chen,* the summer-hunt.—*Zr.*

NOCKAMIXON, (a township in Bucks, bordering on the Delaware), corrupted from *Nochanichsink*,* signifying, *where there are three houses.*

NOLAMÁTTINK,† signifying, *where the silkworm spins,—the silkworm lands,*—was the name given by the Delawares to that part of the "Nazareth tract," on which Gnadenthal and Christian's Spring lay,—and which abounded in the mulberry.

OHIO. (*Note.* Having always failed to satisfy myself that this name was an Indian word, (excepting perhaps as an *abbreviation*), I will proceed to state my views on its probable origin, based upon observation and hearsay, during my residence among the Indians of the Ohio country. There were persons who would have had me believe that *Ohio* signified "*the beautiful river*," and others, "*the river red with blood*," or "*the bloody river.*" This diversity of interpretation exciting my curiosity, I took special care to arrive at a true solution of the problem, by all the means at hand,—by questioning intelligent Indians, and by giving close attention to their conversation, whenever its subject was this river, or any event that had occurred along its course. That an Indian word of but four letters should be so comprehensive as to express the complex idea *beautiful river*, or *bloody river*, I could never concede. Could it even have embraced so much, I was totally at a loss to which of the Indian languages to assign it. The latter designation, furthermore, I knew to be a figurative one, and suggestive of the bloody wars that had been conducted from time immemorial within the country washed by the Ohio and its tributaries.

Only when conversing with traders, or white travelers, to whom the word was familiar, would the Indians, in naming the river in question, call it the *Ohio;* invariably, however, emphasizing the *antepenult*, viz: *O-hi-o*, and *not the penult*, as we do. This circumstance satisfied me that the word was not in the vocabulary of the Lennape or Delawares. Among themselves, the Indians always called the river *Kit-hánne* (in Minsi Delaware, *Gicht-hánne*) which

---

* *Na-cha*, three. *Wik*, a house. *Na che-nach-ke*, thirty. *Zr.*

† *Ne-le-mu-tees*, the silk-worm.—*Zr.* In June of 1752, Philip C. Bader, who was conducting the culture of the silk-worm at Bethlehem, transferred his cocoonery to Christian's Spring, where mention is made of it as late as 1755. *Quaere.* Did the Delawares name the place from this circumstance?

signifies the *main stream*, i. e., in its region of country ;*—a name which is perpetuated in *Kittanning* (once the site of an Indian town on the Allegheny,) corrupted from *Kit-hannink*, signifying *at* or *on the main stream*, i. e., the *town at* or *on the main stream* of its region of country. Thus much for the name of the river in question current among the Delawares,—which name I hold to be the *national* or *historical* one. Next, as to the origin of the name *Ohio* current with us. In tracing this it will be necessary for me to adduce a series of words from the Delaware, all of which have a bearing on the question under consideration. I borrow both from the *Unami* and *Minsi* dialects.

Unami.	*Minsi.*
Ohui, very ; when prefixed, written *Ohi*.	*Achwi*, very.
Opeu, opsit, white.	*Wapeu, wapsit*, white.
Opicchen, it looks white.	*Wapicchen*, it looks white.
Ohiopicchen, it is of a whitish color.	*Wahewapicchen*, it is of a whitish color.
Opeléchen, white, bright.	*Woapeléchen*, white, bright.
Opeek, white with froth.	*Wapeek*, white with froth.
Ohiópeek, very white with froth, or white-caps.	*Achwiwápeek*, very white with froth, or white-caps.
Ohiophánne, a very white stream.	*Achwiwoaphánne*, a very white stream.
Ohiopeekhánne, a very deep and white stream, whitened all over with white-caps.	*Achwiwapeekhánne*, a very deep and white stream, whitened all over with white-caps.

These words, in connection with what I shall proceed to relate, will, I think, be sufficient to convince the reader of the plausibility if not of the correctness of my theory, that the name *Ohio* is only the fragment of an Indian word or words, which in their entirety were used by the Delawares, to describe *a certain condition* of the *main river* (*kit-hanne*) of their western country,—but *not as its name*. The Ohio being often wide, deep and with no perceptible current in its course for miles, the slightest wind that blows up stream, invariably covers its surface with what are provincially called *white-caps*. I have seen the river, when under the influence of a westerly or south-westerly wind, (the prevailing winds of the country) in

---

* See *Kittanning*, in this register.

this condition for several days in succession, so that my Indian companions and myself would be obliged to haul our canoes on shore, well knowing that navigation on the river, when covered with white-caps, was perilous. On such occasions the Indians never failed to apply one or another of the above quoted words to the condition of the river—ejaculating *"juh Ohiopiéchen!"* "Lo! it is of a whitish color!" or, *"Ohiopeek!"* "it is very white!" or *"Ohiophanne!"* "the stream is very white!" and at points where they supposed the river to be very deep, they would exclaim *"Kitschi Ohiopeekhanne!"* i. e., "verily this is a deep and white stream!"

Thus much for the derivation of Ohio. Its fragmentary form is easily accounted for. We owe it to the traders and settlers along the frontiers. The former penetrated the Indian country solely for gain; the latter were generally an illiterate class, and both were satisfied in communicating with the natives, by words (however incorrectly or carelessly spoken) which sufficed to render themselves intelligible. Whenever possible, they would abbreviate Indian words, or adapt them to their powers of enunciation. To such a degree was this corruption of language practised, that the Indians would even indulge in incessant laughter at the quaintness and impropriety of speech made use of by their white visitors.

On their return to the settlements, the traders would report where they had been, and thus ingraft *their* names of streams and places upon the vocabulary of the whites. In this way, I presume to account for the origin of the name *Ohio*.

OHIOPILE, (the falls or rapids of the Youghiogheny in Fayette County), corrupted from *Ohiopéhelle*, signifying, *water whitened by froth* by its rapid descent over rocks and stones.

OLEY, (a township in Berks County), corrupted from *Olink*, or *Olo* (also *Wahlink*, or *Wahlo*,* signifying *a hole, a cavern, a cell*, or "*cache;*" also a cove, that is, a tract of land encompassed by hills.

OSWAYA, (a tributary of the Allegheny in Potter County), corrupted from *Utschéja*,† signifying, *the place of flies.*

PAINT CREEK, (a branch of the Conemaugh or Kiskiminetas,

---

* *Wou-luc,* a hole. *Wal-he-u,* he is digging a hole.—*Zr.*
Oley was one of the first fields of Moravian religious activity in the Province of Pennsylvania.

† *Ut-sche* a fly, *ut-sche-wak,* flies.—*Zr.*

in Cambria County), called by the Delawares *Wallamink*, signifying *where there is paint*.

PAXTON, (emptying into the Susquehanna from the East, at Harrisburg), corrupted from *Peekstank*,* signifying, *where the waters stand*—the place of dead water, whether in a stream, or pool, or lake.

PENNYPACK,† (emptying into the Delaware in Philadelphia County), corrupted from *Pemápeck*, signifying, *a body of water with no current*, whether a stream, a pool, or lake.

PEQUEA,‡ (emptying into the Susquehanna in Lancaster County), corrupted from *Picueu*, a Shawano word.

---

* *Tup-peek*, a spring, a well, standing water. *Hanne*, a stream. *Onk*, *ank*, *ink*, *nk*, and *k*, local suffixes.—*Zr.* The name is written also *Peshtang* and *Pestank* in early official papers. "*July* 25, 1709, the chiefs of several nations living on the Susquehanna at *Peshtang*, *above Conestoga*, met Gov. Gookin in council at Philadelphia." In 1726 John Harris, a Yorkshireman, settled at the mouth of Paxton Creek, traded largely with the Indians by whom he was surrounded, cleared a farm, and kept a ferry. "Harris' Ferry over the Susquehanna," became an important outpost in the Province. John Harris, Jr., born on the Paxton in 1726, inherited from his father 700 acres of land, on a part of which Harrisburg was laid out in 1785. Paxton Township was erected in what was then Lancaster County, in 1729. Its first settlers were Scotch immigrants from the north of Ireland (Scotch-Irish), who, in order to protect their frontier-places against the Indians, on the opening of hostilities, organized a company of rangers. To these belonged the "Paxton Boys" who exterminated the last of the Conestogas on their hereditary seats in Manor Township, Lancaster County, in December of 1763.

† In a letter to James Logan, written at Pennsbury House, the 22d day of 6th month, 1700, Penn directs him in these words, "Urge the Justices about the bridge at *Pemepecka* and *Poquessin* forthwith for a carriage, or I cannot come to town."—*Memoirs of the Historical Society of Penn'a.*, *Vol. IX.* The name of this stream occurs for the first time in deeds, in one executed by four Indian Shakamakers on the 14th day of the 5th month, 1683, to Wm. Penn, for "lands lying between Manaiunk, alias Schuylkill, and *Pemmapeka Creek.*"

‡ Written in early records *Pequehan*, and *Peckquea*, was already before 1707 a settlement of Shawanese (*Southerners* or *South-men*; *Scha-wa-ne-u*, south, *Sha-wa-ne-munk*, southward, *Sha-wa-noch-que* a Shawano woman.—*Zr.*,) at the mouth of the Creek of that name, and the residence of Martin Chartiere, a well-known trader and interpreter, but "late French glover of Philadelphia." When Gov. Evans, in June of 1707, visited the Indians on the Susquehanna, he was conducted to *Pequea* by *Opessah*, the Shawano Chief, and on his entrance into the town saluted by a volley of small arms. Swiss immigrants settled a tract of 10,000 acres on the North side of Pequea Creek in 1710. In order to secure the good will of the neighboring Indians for these strangers, Gov. Gookin met them in conference at Conestoga in June of 1711, and addressed them through Indian Harry, as follows:

PERKIOMEN, a branch of the Schuylkill in Montgomery County), corrupted from *Pakihmomink*,* *Pakiomink*, signifying, *where there are cranberries*, the place of cranberries. *Pakihm*, in Delaware, a *cranberry*.

PINE CREEK, (a branch of the Susquehanna between Lycoming and Clinton Counties.) In Delaware *Cuwenhánne*, i. e., *pine stream* —a stream flowing through pine lands.

PITTSBURG. The Delawares called the site of this city, after its occupation by the French, *Menachk-sink*, which signifies, *where there is a fence*, or an *enclosure*. *Menachk*,† is an enclosed spot of ground, a place secure against entrance, hence equivalent to a *fortification*.

PLAYWICKY,‡ corrupted from *Placuwikichtit*, signifying, *the home or habitation* of Indians of the *Turkey tribe*.

PLUM CREEK, (the North branch of Crooked Creek in Armstrong County.) In Delaware, *Sipuas-hánne*, i. e., *plum stream*. *Sipuássink*, signifies, *where there are plums*.§

POCONO, (emptying into McMichael's Creek in Monroe County), corrupted from *Poco-hánne* signifying, a *stream between mountains*.‖ Broad Mountain received the name *Pocono*, from this creek.

POHOPOCO, or Big Creek, (emptying into the Lehigh from the North-east, in Carbon County), corrupted from *Pochhapochka*, sig-

---

"Gov. Penn on all occasions being willing to show how great a regard he bears to you has sent this small present (50 lbs. of powder, 1 piece of Stroudwaters, 1 piece of duffels and 100 lbs. of shot) to you, and hath required me to acquaint you that he is about to settle some people upon the branches of Potowmack, and doubts not but that the same mutual friendship which has all along as brothers passed between the inhabitants of this government and you, will also continue betwixt you and those he is about to settle. Furthermore he intends to present five belts of wampum to the Five Nations, and one to you of Conestoga, and requires your friendship to the *Palatines settled near Pequea*."

* Occurs the first time in a deed executed by *Manghoughan*, at Philadelphia, the 3d day of 4th month, 1684, in which he makes over all his land on *Pahikihoma* to William Penn, "in consideration of two matchcoats, four pair of stockings, and four bottles of cydar."

† *Mec-nachk*, a fence, a fort. *Me-nach-gink*, in the fence. *Me-nach-gak*, a fence-rail.—*Zr.*

‡ Occurs in the deed of July, 1684, cited under *Makerish-kitton*. *Pla-e-u*, a turkey. *Wik*, a house.

§ *Si-pu-o-man-di-can*, wild plums.—*Zr.*

‖ *Pock-a-wach-ne*, a creek between two hills.—*Zr.*

nifying, *two mountains bearing down upon each other with a stream intervening,*—as is the case at the *Water-gap.**

POKETO, (emptying into the Allegheny from the South, in Allegheny County,) corrupted from *pach gita,*† signifying, *throw it away, abandon it.*

POPONOMING, (a pond, or small lake in Hamilton township, Monroe County), corrupted from *Papennámink,* signifying, *where we are gazing.*

POQUESSING, (emptying into the Delaware between Philadelphia and Bucks Counties), corrupted from *Poquesink,* signifying, *where there are mice,*—the place of mice.‡

PYMATUNING, (a branch of the Chenango in Mercer County), corrupted from *Pihmtomink,*§ signifying *where the man with the crooked mouth resides,*—the home of the man with the crooked mouth. (*Note.* I was acquainted with the person to whose deformity there is allusion in the name of the creek.)

QUAKAKE, (emptying into the Lehigh from the West, in Carbon County), corrupted from *Cuwenkeek,*‖ signifying *pine lands.* *Cuwen-hánne* signifies, *pine-land stream,* i. e., a stream flowing through pine-lands.

QUEMAHONING, (a branch of the Conemaugh or Kiskiminetas, heading in Somerset County), corrupted from *Cuwéi-mahóni,* signifying *pine-tree lick,* i. e., a lick in among pines.

QUENISCHASCHACKI.¶ This name was given by the Delawares

---

* It is inferable from remarks recurring in diaries kept by the Brethren, that the name *Pohopoco* or *Buch-ka-buch-ka* (rock aside of rock, from *gun-schu-puchk,* a rock, in composition abbreviated into *puchk*) was applied to *the region of the Lehigh Water Gap, running back east of the river, and north of the mountain.* Hence it was applied to *the main stream of that region,* now called Big Creek.

† *Pa-ki-ton,* to abandon.—*Zr.*

‡ *Ach-po-quees,* a mouse.—*Zr.* This name occurs in the Record of Upland Court, in a minute of Oct. 8, 1678, recording the survey of a tract of 417 acres of land, situate at the mouth of Pont Quesink Creek, to James Sandelands and Lassie Cock. Also in a release executed by King *Tamanend,* i. e., "the affable," and three other kings, June 15, 1692, at Philadelphia, in which they release to Wm. Penn and his heirs, any further claims on their part to a tract of land situate between Neshaminah and *Poquessing* upon the River Delaware, *claimed by them from the beginning of the world until the aforesaid day.*

§ *Pim-e-u,* slanting. *Pi-moch-que-u,* twisted. *W'doon,* the mouth.—*Zr.*

‖ *Cu-we-u-chae,* pine wood.—*Zr.*

¶ *Quin,* long. *Que-nek,* length. *Schaschuck-ki,* straight.—*Zr.* The Delawares

to the *long reach* in the West Branch of the Susquehanna in Lycoming County. Hence, they called the West Branch *Quenisch-
áchachgek-hánne*, which word has been corrupted into Susquehanna.

QUILUTAMEND, signifying, *we came unawares upon them*, is the
name given by the Delawares to a spot, a short distance above the
mouth of the Lackawannock in Luzerne County, situate between a
steep mountain and the Susquehanna, where, they told me, their
people had surprised and captured a body of Five Nation Indians
(*Mengwe*) in their early wars with that confederacy.

QUITOPAHILLA, (a branch of the Great Swatara in Lebanon
County), corrupted from *Cuitpehelle*, or *Cuwitpehelle*, signifying, *a
spring that flows from the ground among pines.*

RACCOON CREEK, (emptying into the Ohio from the South in
Beaver County). In Delaware, *Nachenum-hanne*,* i. e., *raccoon
stream.*

REDSTONE CREEK, (a branch of the Monongahela in Fayette
County). In Delaware, *Machkachsen-hánne*, i. e., *redstone stream.*†
Machkachsinnink, signifies, *where there are red stones.*

SALT LICK, (a branch of the Youghiogheny in Fayette County.)
In Delaware *Sikhéwi-mahóni.*‡   *Sikei-hánne* signifies a *stream flowing from a salt lick.*

SANDY LICK, (emptying into the Allegheny from the West, in
Venango County.) In Delaware, *Legauwi-mahóni.*

SANKINACK,§ corrupted from *Sank-hánne*, signifying, *flint stream*,
i. e., a stream in or along which flint abounds.

SAUCON, (emptying into the Lehigh from the South-west, in

---

had a town of this name on the *long reach* of the river, said to have stood on the
site of Linden, 6 miles east from Jersey Shore. It was repeatedly visited by missionaries from Bethlehem, prior to 1754. Scull's Map notes it.

* *Na chenum*, a raccoon. *Na-che-num-mook*, raccoons.—*Zr.*

† *Machk-e-u*, red. *Mach-zum-men* to dye red—*machk-te-u*, morning-red—*mach-
gen-ach-gook*, the copper snake. *Ach-sin*, a stone.—*Zr.*

‡ *Si-key*, Salt.—*Zr.*

§ Probably the Delaware name of *Tar Run*, a small stream that empties into
the Lehigh from the West below Weissport, in Carbon County, as may be inferred
from the following extract of a letter written from Bethlehem to Count Zinzendorf
in June of 1747. "As to the improvements at Gnadenhütten—besides completing
the mill-dam and race on the Mahoning, the brethren have thrown a foot-bridge
120 feet long across the *Sankinac, two miles below Gnadenhütten.* By this means
we can communicate with the Mission even in times of freshets, when the Creek
runs wild down the gorge and its passage by raft or canoe is extremely perilous."

Northampton County), corrupted from *Sakunk*,* signifying, *where a smaller stream empties into a larger*, hence, its *place of outlet*. (*Note*. The *outlet of the Big Beaver* into *the Ohio*, a point well known to all Indians,—to warriors of different and of the most distant tribes, as well as of those of the vicinity,—their rendezvous in the French wars,—their thoroughfare and place of transit—a point of observation, and the scene of frequent contest and bloodshed, was the best known of the many *Sakunks*† in the Indian country.)

SCHUYLKILL. The Delawares called the river *Ganshowehánne*,‡ i. e., *the roaring stream*,—the stream that is noisy in its course over rocks and stones.

SERECHEN, corrupted from *Seléhend*, or *Sinuéhund*, signifying, *where milking is done*,—the place of milking.

---

* *Sa-ku-wit*, the mouth of a creek or river.—*Zr.*

† Conrad Weisser in his Journal to the Ohio mentions *Sakunk* under the name of *Beaver Creek*. "August 23, 1748," he writes, "I went to an Indian town *about eight miles below Logstown*, (chiefly Delawares, the rest Mohawks) to have some belts of wampum made." Barbara Lingaree and Mary Roy, who were taken prisoners on John Penn's Creek in Snyder County, in October of 1755, by French Indians, state, in a deposition made on their release from captivity, that they had first been carried to *Kittanning*, thence were removed to Fort Duquesne, thence to *Sakunk*, twenty miles below *at the mouth of the Big Beaver*,—and in the spring of 1757, to *Kaskaskie*, up *Beaver Creek twenty-five miles*." Post, in his Journal to the Ohio records his experience at *Sakunk*, in these words: "Aug. 20, 1758, we set out from *Kaskaskie* for *Sakunk*. My company consisted of twenty-five horsemen and fifteen footmen, and arrived there in the afternoon. The people of this town were very dissatisfied at my coming, and received me in a rough manner. They surrounded me with drawn knives in their hands, so that I could hardly get along, running up against me with their bare breasts, as if they wanted some pretence to kill me. I could read a desire of my life in their countenances,—their faces were quite distorted with rage, and they went so far as to say that I should not live long."

Evans' Map locates *Shingas' Town* at the outlet of the Big Beaver.

‡ *Gan-sche-we-u*, it roars. *Gans-chi-hit-ta-quot*, it makes a terrible noise. *Gan-schi-hi-ta-xen*, a roaring noise.—*Zr.* In old deeds the Schuylkill was called *Manaunk*. Gerrit van Sweeringen, in his "Account of the settling of the Dutch and Swedes at the Delaware," assigns a reason for the name Schuylkill, by stating "that the Swedes' ship sailed up as high as Tinicum, hiding themselves in a creeke, which is called to this day the Schuyl-kill, from *schuylen* to hide, that is, in English the *Hiding Creek*."—*Record of Upland Court.*

Again it is said, that when the Dutch under Capt. Hendricks, sailed up the Delaware in 1616, not knowing whence the river came whose outlet they were passing, they named it Schuylkill, i. e., the hidden kill or stream.

SHACKAMAXON, corrupted from *Schachamesink*,* signifying, *where there are eels*, the place of eels. *Schachameek*, an eel.

SHAMOKIN† (Sunbury) written *Schahamóki*, or *Schahamókink* by the Delawares. In early times the place was called *Schachaméki*, *the place of eels*, and the creek *Schachamékhan*, i. e., *eel-stream*. It was next called *Schachhenamendi*, signifying, *the place where gun barrels are straightened*,‡ because it had become the residence of an ingenious Delaware, *Nutamees*§ by name, who undertook to repair the bent fire-arms of his countrymen.

SHOHOLA, (emptying into the Delaware from the South-west in Pike County) corrupted from *Schauwihilla*,‖ signifying, *weak, faint, depressed*.

SHOHOKIN, (emptying into the Delaware from the South-west in Wayne County,) corrupted from *Schohácan*,¶ signifying *glue*. *Schohacanink*, *where there is glue*, where glue is made.

SHUMMONK,** signifies, *where there is a horn*, the place of the horn.

---

* *Schu chu-meek*, an eel, compounded of *Schu-chach-ge-u*, straight, and *na-mees* a fish,—*the straight fish.—Zr*. Others derive the word from *Sa-ki-ma*, a chief, a king, with the local suffix *ink*, giving it the meaning of *the place of chiefs or kings*, i. e., where sachems meet in council.

† See *Memorials of the Moravian Church, Vol.* 1, *p.* 66, for a further notice of Shamokin, and of the Moravian Mission at that town Pyrlaens, the Iroquois scholar, in a collection of vocables taken from the mouth of the Oneida sachem Shikellimy, while on a visit to Bethlehem in April of 1745, gives *Ot-ze-nach-se*, as the name of the place, in the Maqua, or language of the Six Nations.—*MS. of Iroquois vocables* in possession of the editor.

‡ *Schach-ach-ge-ne-men*, to straighten. *Schach-ach-ga-gee-chen*, a straight road. *Scach ach-ya-me-u*, a straight row.

§ Probably, *old Nutimaes*, one of the signers of "the release for lands on Delaware," executed August 25, 1737, which lands were measured off by the one and a half day's walk in September following. This same Nutimaes, at the time king of Nescopeck, was courteously entertained at Bethlehem in March, 1754, then on his way with his two oldest sons, and negro servants, to the Jerseys. *Pontius Nutimaes* the older son, was born near the site of Philadelphia. Together with his brother *Isaac*, he removed to the Ohio, after the war, and deceased on the Muskingum in 1780. *Nutimaes*, according to Heckewelder, signifies a *spearer of fish*. *Quaere*. Were not perhaps the smithy built at Shamokin by Joseph Powell and John Hagen of Bethlehem in July of 1747, and the blacksmiths Schmid, Wesa and Kieffer, who wrought in iron at that place until in October of 1755,— suggestive of the name *Schach-he-na-men-di* ?

‖ *Schau-we-wi* and *Schau-wi-hit-le-u*, weak. *Shau-wus-su*, he is weak. *Shau-wi-na-zu-woa-gan*, weakness.— *Zr*.

¶ *Sco-ha-can* and *Me-suk-hoa-can*, glue.—*Zr*.

** *W'schum-mo*, a horn. *We-uch-schum-mu-is*, cattle.—*Zr*.

SINNEMAHONING, (emptying into the Susquehanna from the North, in Clinton County), corrupted from *Achsinni-mahoni,** signifying, *stony lick*.

SKIPPACK, (a branch of the Perkiomen in Montgomery County), corrupted from *Schki-peck*,† signifying, *a pool of stagnant, offensive water*.

SLIPPERY ROCK, (emptying into the Big Beaver from the Northeast, in Lawrence County.) In Delaware, *Weschachachápochka,‡* i. e., a *slippery* rock.

STANDING STONE, (emptying into the Juniata from the North, in Huntingdon County) called by the Delawares *Achsinnink, where there is a large stone,§*—the place of the large stone. *Achsinnessink* signifies, *where there is a small stone,*—the place of the small stone. (*Note.* I know of four places within 500 miles called *Achsinnink,* where large stones or rocks stand isolated either on the margin or in the bed of streams.)‖

STONY CREEK, (a branch of the Quemahoning in Somerset County). In Delaware *Sinne-hánne,* or *Achsin-hánne,* i. e., *stony stream*.

---

* *Ach-sün,* a stone, *Ach sün nall,* stones.—*Zr.*

† *Me-nüp-peck,* a pool or pond. *Tup-peck,* a spring or well.

‡ *W'scha-che-u,* slippery.—*Zr.*

§ *Chot-ach sün,* a large rock.—*Zr.*

‖ The *Standing Stone,* a landmark for trader and Indian traveling through the wilds of Western Pennsylvania in the middle of the last century, is first mentioned in records by Weisser in his Journal to Logstown. "Aug. 18, 1748," he writes, "had a great rain in the afternoon, and came within two miles of the Standing Stone." John Harris, in a "report of distances on the road to Logstown," drawn up in 1754, allows "24 miles from Aughwick to the Standing Stone," and observes that "the stone is 14 feet high and 6 inches square." Scull's map locates the pillar on the right bank of the *Achsinnink,* near its outlet, where also stood the Indian village of Standing Stone. When the town of Huntingdon was laid out a few years prior to the Revolution, this historic column was still, though mutilated, at its place. Tradition says that it was a memorial stone, and that on its preservation depended the existence of the tribe who had set it up. Hence when a hostile people once came down the Tuscarora valley, and in the absence of the warriors of Standing Stone carried off their pillar, fierce battles ensued, and there was no peace until the sacred palladium had been restored, and again placed on the flats of the Achsinnink. Three Indian trails diverged from the Standing Stone, one leading to Aughwick, one to Frankstown, and the third to the great Chinklacamoose Path.

There is a Standing Stone in the Susquehanna, opposite the village of that name, in Bradford County.

TAMAQUA. (See Little Schuylkill.)

TIOGA, (one of the tributaries of the Susquehanna, draining Tioga County), corrupted from *Tiaóga*, an Iroquois word, signifying *a gate, a place of entrance.* (*Note.*) This name was given by the Six Nations to the wedge of land lying within the forks of the Tioga and North Branch of Susquehanna,—in passing which streams, the traveler *entered* their territory as *through a gate.* The country south of the forks, was Delaware country. David Zeisberger, who traveled that way to Onondaga in 1750, told me that at *Tiaoga*, or the *Gate*, Six Nation Indians were stationed for the purpose of ascertaining the character of all persons who crossed over into their country, and that whoever entered their territory by another way than through *the Gate*, or by way of the Mohawk, was suspected by them of evil purpose, and treated as a spy or enemy.)*

TOBYHANNA, (emptying into the Lehigh from the North-east in Monroe County, corrupted from *Topi-hánne*, signifying *alder-stream*, i. e. a stream whose banks are fringed with alders.

TOHICKON, (emptying into the Delaware from the West, in Bucks County), corrupted from *Tohickhan*, or *Tohickhánne*, signifying *the drift-wood stream*, i. e., the stream we cross on drift-wood.†

TOWANDA, (emptying into the Susquehanna from the South-west in Bradford County), corrupted from *Tawundeunk*, signifying

---

* Bishop Spangenberg, accompanied by David Zeisberger and John Shebosh, passed through the Gates of Tioga, on the 12th of June, 1745, on the way to Onondaga. They were the first Moravians to enter the country of the Six Nations at this point of ingress. Spangenberg states, that they were there distant from Shamokin, about 180 miles by water, and were come to a Mohican town.

† This stream, heading not far below the outliers of the South Mountain or "Lechay Hills," (up to which point the Indian claims had been extinguished) was repeatedly declared by Teedyuscung, the Delaware King, to be the southern limit of the white man's country, and he furthermore asserted that all lands lying between the Tohickon and Wyoming had been fraudulently taken from him and his people, and were in the occupancy of intruders.

"I desire to see T. Fairman, for that I hear an Indian township called *Tohickon*, rich land, and much cleared by the Indians, he has not surveyed to mine and children's tracts, as I expected. It joins upon the back of my manor of Highlands, and I am sorry my Surveyor-general did not inform me thereof. If it be not in thy warrants, put it in, except lands already or formerly taken up, or an Indian township. The Indians have been with me about it." *Wm. Penn to James Logan, Pennsbury, 6th day, 7th month,* 1700. Penn and Logan correspondence.

where we bury the dead. (*Note.*) Here the Nanticokes buried the bones of their dead.

TOWSISSIMOCK,* corrupted from *Dawá-simook*, signifying, *the feeding place of cattle*, i. e., pasture grounds.

TOMBICON,† corrupted from *Tombic-hanne*, signifying, *crab-apple stream*.

TUCQUAN, corrupted from *P'duc-hanne*,‡ signifying, a *winding stream*; corrupted from *p'ducquan*, round, and *hanne* a stream. *P'ducachtin* signifies a *round hill* or *knoll*.

TULPEHOCKEN, (a branch of the Schuylkill in Berks County), corrupted from *Tulpewi-hacki*,§ signifying, *the land of turtles*.

TUNKHANNA, (a branch of the Tobyhanna in Monroe County),

---

* The name occurs in the deed of July, 1682, cited under *Makerisk-kitton*.

† *Tom-bi-ca-nall*, crabs, or wild apples.—*Zr.* Tombican Creek occurs under the head of Berks and Schuylkill in Heckewelder's arrangement. *Quaere.*—*Tumbling Run*, a branch of the Schuylkill at Pottsville?

‡ *P'tnck-hi-can*, a ball. *P'tuck-han-ne*, a bend in a stream. *P'tuck-quin-schu*, a round bowl.—*Zr.*

§ *Tul-pe*, a water or sea-turtle. *Tach-quoch*, a land-turtle. *Hac-ki*, the earth, the land.—*Zr.* During Mr. Heckewelder's stay among the Delawares of the Muskingum in the summer of 1762, he received the name of *Pi-se-la-tul-pe*. *Quaere*, compounded of *Pi-se lüs-so*, wrinkled, and *tul-pe*, a turtle?

In March of 1705 the Conoys requested permission of Geo. Evans to remove from their towns on the Susquehanna to *Tulpehocken*. In July of 1707 the Governor visited the Indian town of Tulpehocken, which tradition locates near the site of Womelsdorf, in Berks County.

The lands watered by Tulpehocken Creek and its tributaries, were settled by Germans from Scoharie (without the knowledge of the Proprietaries' agents, and before the Indian claim had been bought) in 1723. Among these Palatines were the Weisser's and George Loesch, the ancestor of the Moravian family of Loesch or Lash. This unwarrantable occupation much dissatisfied the Indians, and was made a matter of complaint by the Delaware chiefs Sassoonan and Opekasset, at a conference with Gov. Gordon, held at Philadelphia in June of 1728. The Indian claim was bought by Thomas Penn soon after his arrival in the country, in 1733. Tulpehocken was one of the rural districts of the Province in which the Brethren labored in the Gospel, with marked success. Zinzendorf preached there frequently, and in the spring of 1742, Gottlieb Büttner of Bethlehem, was on his recommendation accepted by the settlers as their minister. They hereupon built him a church. Philip Meurer succeeded Büttner in the autumn of the year, and the Brethren were inclined to believe that they had now effected a permanent footing; but as a Lutheran church was organized in the neighborhood (this was in 1743) they lost influence, were regarded with distrust, and then with displeasure, and finally (in January of 1747) deprived of the building in which they worshipped. Meurer was accordingly recalled to Bethlehem.

corrupted from *Tank-hanne*,* i. e., *the small stream.* (*Note.* The smallest of two or more confluents or sources of a river is always called *tank-hanne* by the Delawares.) *Tunkhannock* is a corruption of the same.

TUPPEEKHÁNNA, (one of the sources of the Little Lehigh at Trexlertown, in Upper Macungy, Lehigh County). The word signifies *the stream that flows from a large spring.*

TURTLE CREEK, (emptying into the Monongahela from the East, in Allegheny County). The Delawares called it *tulpewisipu,* i. e., *turtle river.*

TWO LICKS, (a branch of the Conemaugh in Indiana County). In Delaware *Nischa-hóni,* i. e., *two licks.*

VENANGO. The Delawares called French Creek *Attike.* (*Note.* The name was sometimes written *Onenge.*)

WAPPASUNING, (a branch of the Susquehanna in Bradford County), corrupted from *Wapachsinnink,*† signifying, *where there are white stones,* alluding to a deposit of silver ore—the Delaware for silver being *Woap-áchsin,* i. e., *the white stone.*

WAPWALLOPEN, or Whopehawly,‡ (emptying into the Susquehanna from the East in Luzerne County), corrupted from *Woaphallách-pink,* signifying, *where the white hemp grows,* i. e., the kind, which when dressed, is whitest.

WAULLENPAUPACK, or Paupack, (a branch of the Lackawaxen, dividing Wayne and Pike Counties,) corrupted from *Walinkpapeek,*§ signifying, *deep and dead water.*

WECHQUETANK, for *Wekquitank,* the Delaware name of a species of willow, growing in the neighborhood of the Indian town of that name, once on Head's Creek, (*Hoeth's* Creek) in Monroe County.‖

---

* *Tang-han-ne-u,* a little stream, or run.—*Zr.*

† *Woap,* white. *Woap-ach-poan,* white-bread. *Woap-i-min schi,* the white tree, i. e., the chestnut tree, because white when covered with blossoms.—*Zr.*

‡ This name is invariably written *Wambhallobank* by Moravian Missionaries. Gottlieb and Mary, the first converts from the Delawares, who were united with the Church by baptism, administered at Bethlehem, in April of 1745, resided on the Wapwallopen.

§ *Woa lac,* a hole. *Me-nü-peek,* a pool.—*Zr.*

‖ The seat of a Moravian Mission, between April of 1760, and October of 1763, part of the Christian Indians at Bethlehem, last from Gnadenhütten, having been transferred thither, at the first named date.

WELAGAMIKA,* signifying, *rich soil*, was the name of a Delaware town on the "Nazareth tract," when the Moravians came there in 1740. The Indians applied the name to the entire tract.

WHEELING CREEK, (heading in Washington County), corrupted from *Wihling*, or *wih-link*, signifying, *where the head is*, or *the place of the head.*† (*Note.* The Indians state that along this creek they had decapitated a prisoner, and then impaled his head).

WHITE DEER, (emptying into the Susquehanna from the West, in Union County). In Delaware, *Woap'tuchánne*, i. e., *white-deer stream.*‡

WICONISCO, (emptying into the Susquehanna from the East in Dauphin County), corrupted from *Wikenkniskeu*, signifying, a *wet and muddy camp.*§ (*Note.* Probably some Indians encamped along the creek, where the bank was wet and muddy.)

WINGOHOCKING, (the South branch of Frankford Creek), corrupted from *Wingehacking*,‖ signifying, *a favorite spot for planting.*

WISSAHICKON, corrupted from *Wisameekhan*,¶ signifying, *catfish stream.*

WISSINOMING, (the Tacony, or North branch of Frankford Creek), corrupted from *Wischánemunk*,** *where we were frightened.*

WOLF CREEK, (a branch of the Slippery Rock in Mercer County), called by the Delawares *Tummeink*, signifying,†† *where there is a wolf*, i. e., *the place of wolves.*

WYALUSING, (emptying into the Susquehanna from the Northeast in Bradford County), corrupted from *M'chwihilusing*,‡‡ signifying, *the place of the hoary veteran.*

---

* *Weh-lick*, the best. *Hacki*, land. *Ha-cka-mi-ga*, a small tract of land. *Ha-gi-ha-can*, a plantation. *Linn-ha-cka-mi-ga*, common land, *Kit-ha-cka-mi-ga*, upland, *Si-ap-ha-cka-mi-ge-u*, wet land.

This village was reluctantly abandoned by *Captain John* in the autumn of 1742.

† *Wihl*, the head. *Wi-tünk*, on the head.—*Zr.*

‡ *Woap-su* and *Wou-peek*, white. *Ach-tu*, a deer. *Ach-tu-hu*, where deer are plenty.—*Zr.*

§ *Wik* and *wi-quoam*, a house. *Wi-quoam-tit*, a small house. *Nisk-as-sis-ku*, muddy. *Nisk-su*, nasty. *Gun-das-sis-ku*, mire.—*Zr.*

‖ *Win-gan*, sweet. *Ha-gi-ha-can*, a plantation.—*Zr.*

¶ *Wi-su*, fat, fleshy. *Na-mees*, a fish.—*Zr.*

** *Wi-schas-sin*, to be afraid.—*Zr.*

†† *Tim-me-u* and *Me-tum-me-u*, a wolf.—*Zr.*

‡‡ *Mi-hi-lu-sis*, an old man. *Mi-hi-lu-sac* and *Mi-hil-lu-sis-sac*, old men.—*Zr.*

The first Moravians to cross the Wyalusing in "the land abounding in the

Wyoming,* corrupted from *M'cheuomi*, or *M'cheuwami*, signifying *extensive flats*. The North Branch of Susquehanna was in consequence called *M'cheuwcami-sipu*, i. e., *the river of the extensive flats*. The Iroquois called it *Gahonta*, a word of like signification.

Wysox, or Wysaukin, (emptying into the Susquehanna from the North-east in Bradford County), corrupted from *Wisachgimi*,† signifying, *the place of grapes*.

Yellow Breeches, (a branch of the Susquehanna dividing

---

sugar tree" (*ach-sân-na-minschi*), were Bishop Cammerhoff and David Zeisberger, on the way to Onondaga in the summer of 1750. In July of 1759, a Monsey of Wyalusing, one *Papoonhank*, while visiting acquaintances at Nain, near Bethlehem, was deeply impressed by the preaching of the Gospel, so that on his return to his people, (with whom he stood in high repute as a teacher of morality), his representations of what he had lately heard, prepared their minds for the reception of Christianity. Thus it came to pass that David Zeisberger missionated at Wyalusing in 1763, and that Papoonhank was admitted into the Christian Church, by baptism, on the 26th of June of that year. The Monsey village of Wyalusing, or Papoonhank's town, is thus described by John Hays in his Journal to Tioga: "*May* 19, 1760. Arrived at a town called *Quihiloosing*. The captain's name is *Wampomham*, a very religious civilized man, in his own way, who showed us a great deal of kindness. The town is on the Susquehanna, east side, about twenty houses full of people, very good land and good Indian buildings, all new." Post, who accompanied Hays, writes in his report, "which is endorsed," Frederic Post's relation of what passed between him and the Quaker or religious Indians at *Monmuchlooson* on the Susquehanna," as follows: "Dear Sir,—It gives me great pleasure to inform your honor of our arrival at *Machhachlosung*, an Indian town *newly laid out*, where there dwells a company of Monseys, a religious people in their way. It is about eight years since they were gathered together by *Papoonhang*, who is their leader and teacher."

In Dec. of 1763, Papoonhank (who in baptism had received the name of *John*) came to Bethlehem with twenty-one of his Monsey adherents, desirous of sharing the protection which Government was in that perilous time extending to all friendly Indians. In this way the chieftain and his company came to be incorporated with the Moravian Indians, whom they cheerfully followed into exile to Philadelphia. On the return of peace, it was John Papoonhank, who offered to intercede in person with the Six Nations, in behalf of his Christian brethren for permission to plant on the site of the Monsey town on the Wihilnsing. This was granted, and so it came to pass that in the spring of 1765, *Friedenshütten* (huts of peace) was built by the Moravian Indians under Schmick and Zeisberger. Wyalusing was deserted by the Moravian Indians in June of 1772.

* For a further notice of Wyoming, see *Memorials of the Moravian Church*, Vol. I, *p.* 69.

† *Wi-sach-gau*, bitter, pungent. *Wi-sach-gim*, grapes. *Wi-sach-gi-min-schi*, the grape-vine. *Wi-sach-gank*, rum.—*Zr.*

Cumberland and York Counties). The Delawares called it *Cal-lapátschink*, signifying, *where it returns*, in allusion to a point in the creek's course where it bends back.

YOUGHIOGHENY, (a branch of the Monongahela in Fayette County), corrupted from *Juh-wiah-hanne*, signifying, *a stream flow-ing in a contrary direction*, or in a circuitous course.

2. DELAWARE NAMES

OF RIVERS, STREAMS AND LOCALITIES IN NEW JERSEY.

ACHQUAKENUNA, corrupted from *Tachquahacanéna*, signifying, *where pounding-blocks or mortars, are made*,—where the gum tree (*Tachquacheaniminschi*) grows, of whose wood hominy-blocks are made.

AMBOY, corrupted from *Emboli*, signifying, *round, hollow*. *Em-boolhatton*, signifies, " *hollow it out.*" When speaking of this place, the Indians would say *Embolink*, i. e., *where there is a hollow, or at the hollow place*. (*Note*. An old Indian, born on the site of Amboy, about 1680, with whom I was acquainted for upwards of twenty years, informed me, that as the spot resembled a *bowl*, it was called *Emboli*.

CHYGOES, (the island in the Delaware opposite Burlington), called by the Indians *T'schichopacki*, signifying, *the oldest planted ground*. *Note*. The Delawares state that their first settlement so far east, was on this island.

HACKENSACK, corrupted from *Hackinksaquik*, signifying, *a stream that unites with another on low ground*, or *imperceptibly*.

HOBOKEN, corrupted from *Hopócan*,* *a tobacco-pipe*.

MACKIAPIER, corrupted from *Machkkiiibi*, signifying, *reddish water.*†

MUSCONETCONG, corrupted from *Maskhanneunk*, *a rapid stream*.

PASSAIC, corrupted from *Pasáic*, or *Passajeck*, signifying, *a val-ley*.

---

* *Ho-poa-can*, a pipe.—*Zr.*
† *Mach-ke-u*, red. *M'bi*, water.—*Zr.*

7

PISCATAWAY, corrupted from *Pisgattauwi,* signifying, *it is growing dark.**

POGUNNOCK, corrupted from *Peck-hanne,* signifying, *the dark stream.†*

POMPTON, corrupted from *Pihmtoon,* signifying, *crooked-mouthed.‡*

ROMOPACK, corrupted, probably, from *Walumipeck,§* a *round pond, or lake.*

SUSPECAUGH, corrupted from *Sispeckh,║* signifying, *muddy standing water.*

TAPPAN, corrupted from *Tuppeck-hanne,* signifying, *a stream issuing from a large spring.*

TOTAWA FALLS. Totawa corrupted from *Totauwei,* signifying, *to dive and reappear.*

WALPACK, corrupted from *Wahlpeck,¶* signifying a *turn-hole.*

WANTAGE, corrupted from *Wundachqui,*** signifying, *that way.*

WHIPPANY, corrupted from *Wip-hanne,* signifying, *arrow-stream,* i. e., a stream along which the *arrow-wood* grows.

WISCONK, corrupted from *Wis-quonk,* signifying, *where there is an elbow. Wisquoan* signifies a *twist,* anything *twisted,* as a *twist* of yarn, or a *twist* of tobacco.

---

* *Pis-ge-ke,* night. *Pis-ge-u,* it is night. *Pischk,* the night-hawk.—*Zr.*

† *Pe-ge-nünk,* in darkness.—*Zr.*

‡ See *Pymatuning* in this Register.

§ *Woa-lac,* a hole, *Wa-lum-eu,* round. *Tup-peck,* a pool.—*Zr.*

║ *Nisk-as-sis-ku,* muddy. *Tuppeck,* a pool.—*Zr.*

¶ Compounded of *Woa-lac,* a hole, and *tuppeck,* a pool. The name *turn-hole,* a provincialism now obsolete, was used to designate a sudden bend of a stream around the base of a rock, by which means the water when deep was turned upon itself into an eddy. Sixty years ago the *Turn Hole* in the Lehigh, above Mauch Chunk, was one of the objects of interest, which attracted the attention of travelers in that then wild region of country.—Howel's Map of 1792, indicates the spot.

** *Wa-li,* yonder. *Wum,* he came thence. *Wun-dach-al,* come here.—*Zr.*

3. DELAWARE NAMES

OF RIVERS, STREAMS AND PLACES IN MARYLAND.

ACQUIA, corrupted from *Equiwi*,* signifying, *between*.

AQUAKIK, corrupted from *Achowékik*, signifying, *a thicket*.

AQUÁSQUIT, corrupted from *Achowasquit*, signifying, *grassy, overgrown with grass*.

CHESAPEAKE, corrupted from *Tschischwapeki*, or *K'tschischwapecki*,, compounded of *Kitschi*, signifying, *highly salted*, and *peck*, a body of *standing water*, *a pond*, *a bay*.

CHICKNICOMIKA, corrupted from *Tschikenumiki*,† signifying, *the place of turkeys*.

CORAPECHEN, corrupted from *Colapéchen*, signifying, *a fine running stream*.

MAGOTTY, corrupted from *Megukty*, signifying a *small plain destitute of timber*, a *meadow*, or *prairie*.

MANOKIN, corrupted from *Menáchkink*,‡ signifying an *enclosed spot*, whether a *fort*, or a *town*.

MESONGO, corrupted from *Meschánge*,§ signifying, *where we kill deer*.

NANTICOKE, corrupted from *Néchticok*. (*Note*. Along this stream the Nanticokes, who are descendants of the Delawares, had their settlements.)

OCCOQUAN, corrupted from *Okhucquoan*,‖ a *hook*, *a pot hook*.

OPICON, corrupted from *Opeckhan*, signifying, *a stream of whitish color*.

PAMUNKY, corrupted from *Pihmunga*,¶ signifying, *where we sweat*, viz: in the sweat-house.

---

* *Equi-wi*, under.—*Zr.*

† *Tschi-ke-num*, a turkey.—*Zr.*

‡ *Me-nach-günk*, within the fence.—*Zr.*

§ *Me-scha-can*, to wound.—*Zr.*

‖ *Hoc-quoan*, a pot-hook.—*Zr.*

¶ *Pihm*, to sweat. *Pomo-a-can*, a sweat-house. *Pimook*, go to sweat. *Pim-hottin*, they are sweating.

"The Indians are remarkably addicted to the use of sweating-baths, made of earth and lined with clay. A small door serves as an entrance. The patient creeps in, seats himself and places heated stones around the sides. Whenever he has sweated a certain time, he immerses himself suddenly in cold water; from which he derives great security against all sorts of sickness."—*Beschryving von America on t' Zuidland, door Arnoldus Montanus, Amsterdam* 1671.

"Their physic is scarcely anything beyond a hot-house or a powaw. Their hot-house is a little cave, where, after they have terribly heated it, a crew of them go and sit and sweat and smoke for an hour together, and then immediately run into some cold adjacent brook, without the least mischief to them."—*Increase Mather.*

"The sweating-houses of the Indians of Carolina and Florida, are usually placed on the banks of rivers, and are some of stone and some of clay. In form and size they are like a large oven, into which they roll stones heated very hot. The patient creeps into the chamber thus prepared, and is closely shut up. After about an hour's confinement in this warm situation, he comes forth all reeking in torrents of sweat and plunges into the river. Among the benefits which they receive by this sweating, they say it cures fevers, dissipates pains in the limbs contracted by colds, also rheumatic diseases, and creates fresh spirits and agility, enabling them the better to hunt."—*Catesby's Natural History of Carolina, Florida and the Bahama Islands.*

"In those complaints which proceed from rheumatic affections, bleeding and *sweating* are always the first remedies applied. The *sweat-oven* is the first thing an Indian has recourse to, when he feels the least indisposed; it is the place to which the weary traveler, hunter or warrior looks for relief from the fatigues he has endured, the cold he has caught, or for the restoration of his lost appetite.

"The oven is made of different sizes so as to accommodate from two to six persons at a time, or according to the number of men in the village, so that they may be all successively served. It is generally built on a bank or slope, one half of it within and the other above ground. It is well covered on the top with split planks and earth, and has a door in front, where the ground is level, to go or rather creep in. Here, on the outside, stones, generally of about the size of a large turnip, are heated by one or more men appointed each day for that purpose. While the oven is heating, decoctions from roots or plants are prepared either by the person himself who intends to sweat, or by one of the men of the village, who boils a large kettleful for general use, so that when the public crier going his rounds, calls out "*Pimook!*" "*go to sweat!*" every one brings his small kettle which is filled for him with the potion, which at the same time serves him as a medicine, promotes a profuse perspiration, and quenches his thirst. As soon as a sufficient number have come to the oven, hot stones are rolled into the middle of it, and the sweaters go in, seating themselves or rather squatting around the stones, and there they remain until the sweat ceases to flow; then they come out, throwing a blanket or two about them that they may not catch cold. In the meantime, freshly heated stones are thrown in for those who follow them. While they are in the oven, water is now and then poured on the hot stones to produce steam, which they say increases the heat, and gives suppleness to their limbs and joints. In rheumatic complaints, the steam is produced by a decoction of boiled roots and the patient during the operation is well wrapped up in blankets to keep the cold from him, and promote perspiration at the same time.

Sweat-ovens are generally at some distance from the village, and where wood

PATAPSCO, corrupted from *Petapsqui*,* signifying, *back-water*, or *tide-water covered with froth.*

PICCOWAXEN, corrupted from *Pixáwaxen*,† or *Pikiuwaxen*, signifying, *torn-shoes.*

POKOMOKA, corrupted from *Pocqucumoke*, the place of shell-fish.‡

POTOMAC, corrupted from *Pethamook*, signifying, *they are coming by water.*

QUENTICO, corrupted from *Gentican*,§ signifying, *dancing*, the place of dancing.

QUEPONCO, corrupted from *Cuwenpónga*,‖ signifying, *ashes of pine-wood.* (*Note.* Probably some Indians encamping on the bank of this stream, were necessitated to bake their bread in such ashes.)

SASSAFRAS RIVER. In Delaware, *Winak-háune*,¶ i. e., sassafras stream.

SENEGAR CREEK, corrupted from *Sinnike*, signifying, *stony*, *Sinni-hanne*, a *stony stream.*

SENEGAR FALLS. In Delaware, *Sinnipehelle*, i. e., *water running over stones.*

SHENANDOAH, corrupted from *Schindhandowi*, or *Schindhando-wik*,** signifying, *the sprucy stream*, i. e., a stream flowing past spruce-pines.

TUCKAHOE, corrupted from *Tucháchowe*, signifying, *deer are shy. Tuchá-uchoak, the place where deer are shy.*

WILIPQUIN,†† right Delaware, signifying, *the place of interring*

---

and water are at hand. The best order is preserved at these places. The women have a separate oven in a different direction from that of the men, and subjected to the same rules. The men generally sweat themselves once and sometimes twice a week; the women have no fixed day for this exercise, nor do they take it as often as do the men."—*Heckewelder's Indian Nations*, p. 219.

* *Pe-ta quic-chen*, the water is rising.— *Zr.*
† *Pix-u*, ragged. *Muck-sen*, a shoe or sock.—*Zr.*
‡ *Poc-que-u*, a clam, a mussel.—*Zr.*
§ Hence, *cantico*, an Indian dance. See note under *Hascanawpen*, in this register.
‖ *Pongus*, the sand-fly,—ashes.—*Zr.*
¶ *Wi-nakch*, the sassafras tree.— *Zr.*
** *Schind*, the spruce tree. *Schin di-ke-u*, where spruce is plenty.—*Zr.*
†† *Wihl*, the head.—*Zr.*

skulls. (*Note.* The Nanticokes had a custom of carrying the *skulls* and even the bones of their deceased to certain places, where they buried them in caverns or holes.)

WICOMICO, corrupted from *Wikcomika,** signifying, *where houses are building.*

·   ———

4. INDIAN NAMES

OF RIVERS, STREAMS, LOCALITIES AND PERSONS,

COPIED FROM AN EARLY HISTORY OF VIRGINIA,† ALL WHICH NAMES, BEING DELAWARE, ARE EVIDENCE THAT THE LENNAPE WERE IN POSSESSION OF THAT COUNTRY WHEN FIRST OCCUPIED BY THE ENGLISH.

ACCOMACK, corrupted from *Achgameek,* signifying, *a broad bay.*

ARRAHATUK, corrupted from *Allahatteek,* signifying, *empty, there is no more of it;* spoken probably of a bottle, keg or vessel, *emptied* of its liquor.

CHAPACOUR, corrupted from *Tscháppichk,* a medicine prepared from *roots,—tscháppick,* signifying, *a root.*

CHICKAHOMINY, corrupted from *Tschikenemahoni,* signifying, *a turkey-lick, a lick* frequented by *turkeys.* (*Note.* I know several places that bear this name)

CHICONNESSE, corrupted from *Chiconásink,* signifying, *where it was forcibly taken from us.*"

CHISSENESSICK, corrupted from *T'schuissenetschik,* signifying, *the place of blue birds.*‡

GANGASCOE, corrupted from *Shingáscui,* signifying, *level and boggy.*§

---

* *Wik* and *wi-quoam,* a house. *Wik-i-a,* my house. *Wi-kich-tid,* their house. *Wi-ke-u,* he is building a house.— *Zr.*

† *The History of Virginia, in four parts, by a native and inhabitant of the place. London,* 1705.

‡ *Tschi-ma-lus,* and *Tschi-hou-pe-ke-lis,* the blue bird.— *Zr.*

§ *Shin-ge-u,* level. *Shin-gas-gunk,* a bog-meadow.— *Zr.* Shingas was the name of a brother of King Beaver, one of the ablest war-chiefs of the western Delawares, between 1755 and 1763.

GINGOTEQUE, corrupted from *Shinghattéke*, signifying, *he rejects it, he despises it.**

HUSCANAWPEN, corrupted from *Hus-ca-na-pe-i*, or rather, *husca n'lenapewi*, signifying, *Indeed I am a Lennape!*† an *Indian of the original stock!*—an exclamation or refrain I often heard the Delawares use at their *Canticoes* or festive dances.‡

KIEQUOTANK, corrupted from *Kiwiquótank*, signifying, *a risitor.*§

KIQUOLAN, corrupted from *Kiquatank*, signifying both, *one who heals*, and *the place where the sick are healed.*||

MACOCK, corrupted from *Mitzhack*, the name given by the Delawares to the edible kinds of hard-shelled fruits or pepones, such as the *pumpkin*, the *cashaw*, &c., compounded of *mitz*, (from *mitzin*, to *eat*) and *hack*, *rind* or *shell*. *Hackhack* is their word for *gourd*. Each variety of pepo has its specific name. *Geskondháckan* is the generic name. (*Note.* The boxes made from the inner bark of the elm or birch, in which the Indians pack maple-sugar for transportation, are also called *macocks*.)¶

---

* *Schin-gat-tam*, to dislike. *Shin-ga-lend*, one who is disliked.—*Zr.*

† *Le-na-pe*, an Indian. *Lenapewak*, Indians. *Lin-ni le-na-pe*, Indians of the same nation.—*Zr.*

‡ "Their *Canticoes*, as they call them, are performed by round dances, sometimes words, then songs, then shouts,—two being in ye middle that begin and direct ye chorus. This they perform with great fervency and appearances of joy." *Wm. Penn to Henry Savell, Phil'a., 30th day, 5th month, 1683.*

"It is a pleasing spectacle to see the Indian dances, when intended merely for social diversion and innocent amusement. I acknowledge I would prefer being present at them for a full hour, than a few minutes only at such dances as I have witnessed in our country taverns among the white people. Their songs are by no means unharmonious. They sing in chorus, first the men and then the women. At times the women join in the general song, or repeat the strain which the men have just finished. It seems like two companies singing in questions and answers, and is upon the whole very agreeable and enlivening. After thus singing for about a quarter of an hour, they conclude with a loud yell, which I confess is not in concord with the rest of the music. One person always begins the singing; others fall in successively, and then comes the chorus, the drum beating all the while to mark the time. The voices of the women are clear and full, and their intonations generally correct."—*Heckewelder's Indian Nations.*

§ *Ki-wi-ke*, to visit. *Ki-wi-ke-u*, he visits. *Ki-wi-ka-mell*, I visit you. *Ki-wi-ka-mi*, visit me.—*Zr.*

|| *Ki-ke-woa-gan*, a cure.—*Zr.*

¶ *Mit-zin*, to eat. *Mitz-u*, he eats. *Mit-zit te*, if he eat. *Mi-ziech-tit*, their victuals. *Ge-scund-hac*, pumpkins.—*Zr.*

MATCHACOMOCA, corrupted from *Matachgenimoah*, signifying, *they are counselling about war,—they are holding a council of war,—* hence also a *council of war.*

MATCHOPUNGO, corrupted from *Matschipungo*, signifying *bad powder*, or *bad ashes* (i. e., ashes unfit for the baking of bread).*

MATOMKIN, corrupted from *Mattemikin*, signifying, *to enter a house.*†

MATTAPONY, corrupted from *Mattachpóna*,‡ signifying, *no bread at all—no bread to be had!*

MENHEERING, corrupted from *Menhattink*, signifying, *on the island.*§

MOCCASIN, corrupted from *Macksen*, Delaware for *shoe* or *sock.*‖

MONACAN, corrupted from *Monhácan*, a *spade*, or any implement used for digging the soil.

NANSAMOND, corrupted from *Neunschimend*, signifying, *whence we fled.*

NEMATTANO, corrupted from *Nimmattima*, signifying, *our brother. Ni-mat*, a brother.

OAKSUSKIE, corrupted from *Woak-as-sisku*, signifying, *a winding marsh or bog.*¶

OANANCOCK, corrupted from *Awrannáku*, signifying, *foggy.***

OCCOHANNOCK, corrupted from *Woak-hanne, a winding stream.*

OPPEEHANEANOUGH, corrupted from *Opcek-hánne, a froth-white stream*, or from *Huppecehk-hanne, the rain-worm stream, huppecehk*, signifying, *a rain worm.*

---

* *Mach-tis-s-isu*, and *mach-tit-su*, bad. *Pungus*, ashes.—*Zr.* The bread used by the Indians is of two kinds; one made of green corn while in the milk, and another of the same grain when fully ripe and dry. This last is pounded as fine as possible, then sifted and kneaded into dough, and afterwards made up into cakes of six inches diameter, and an inch in thickness rounded off on the edge. In baking these cakes, they are extremely particular. *The ashes must be clean and hot, and if possible come from good dry oak bark, which they say gives a good and durable heat.* The Indians laugh at the white hunters for baking their bread in dirty ashes."—*Heckewelder's Indian Nations.*

† *Mat-te-mi-geen*, to enter in.—*Zr.*

‡ *Met-ta*, no. *Ach-poan*, bread.—*Zr.*

§ *Me-na-tey*, an island, *ink*, the local suffix.—*Zr.*

‖ *Wusk-ha-zen*, new shoes; compounded of *wus-ken*, new, and *muck-sen*, shoes.—*Zr.*

¶ *Woak-tschin-i*, to bend. *Woak-tsche-u*, crooked. *Woak-tschuch ne*, compounded of *Woaktscheu* and *hanne*, a bend in a river. *Nisk-as-sis-ku*, muddy.—*Zr.*

** *A-wonn*, fog.

PAMUNKY, corrupted from *Pihmunga*, signifying, *where we sweat*.

POCCOSEN, corrupted probably from *P'duckassin*,[*] signifying, *a place where balls, bullets or lead are to be had*.

POCOHONTAS, corrupted from *Pockohantes*, signifying, *a stream-let or run between two hills*, compounded of *pochko*, a rock, or rocky hill, and *hanne*, a stream, the latter word made a diminutive by the suffix *tes*.[†]

POCOMOKE, corrupted from *Pockhammökik*, signifying, *broken or diversified by knolls and hills*.

POWHATÁN, corrupted from *Pawai-hánne*, i. e., *the stream of wealth or fruitfulness*,[‡] the name of *James River* as well as of the historic sachem of the allied Powhatans.

PUNGOTEQUE. (*Note.* The Delaware word *pung*, signifies, *powder*, and also, *ashes*, *dust* and *fine sand*. The word as above incorrectly written may denote a locality where either of those substances abound. Written *Punghatteke*, it denotes *the place of powder*.

RAPPAHANNOCK, corrupted from *Lappi hánne*,[§] signifying, *the stream with an ebb and flow*. *Lappahanniuk*, signifies, *where the tide-water flows and ebbs*.

TANGOMOCKONOMINGO, corrupted from *Tangamochkomenúnga*, signifying, "*the bark for the medicine*," which was brought from Little Beaver Creek, (*Tangamochke*).

TOMAHAWK, corrupted from *Tamahican*, an *axe* or *hatchet*.

UTTAMACCOMACK, corrupted from *Uchtamáganal*, signifying, *a path-maker, a leader*. (*Note.* The name of a well known war-chief.)

WASEBUR, corrupted from *Waschábuck*, signifying, *a physic*.

---

[*] *Al-uns* and *P'tuck-a-tuns*, a bullet. *Al-uns-ha-can*, a bullet mould.—*Zr*.

[†] *Pock-ka-wach-ne*, a stream between two hills.—*Zr*.

Pocohontas, daughter of Powhatan, well-known for her friendship to the early colonists of Virginia, was born about 1595. Soon after her baptism in which she received the name of *Rebecca*, she married John Rolfe, of Jamestown, in April of 1613. In 1616 she went to England, where she was an object of great interest to all classes, and was presented at Court by Lady De la Ware. When on the point of embarking on her return to America, she died at Gravesend, in March of 1617. She left one son. John Randolph of Roanoke, was descended from Pocahontas on his father's side,—other descendants are still found in Virginia.

[‡] *Pa-wall-si*, to be rich.—*Zr*.

[§] *Lap-pe*, again. *Lap-pech-si*, to tell it over again.—*Zr*.

8

Werauwano, corrupted probably from *Wajaúwi*, Minsi Delaware for *chief*.

Wighsacan, corrupted from *Wisachgim, sour grapes*, or from *Wisachgank, rum*, or *whiskey*, *wisachk* signifying, *pungent* to the taste.

Wigwam, corrupted from *wiquoam, a house*.

Winank, corrupted from *winaak*, the *sassafras tree*.

Wisoccon, corrupted from *wisachcan*, signifying, anything *bitter* or *pungent* to the taste.

Wyanoke, corrupted from *Wigunáka*, signifying, *the point of an island—the land's end*.